BAD PENNY

JOSH GENTRY

SNACK READS PRESS

HELP A WRITER OUT

I f you enjoy the story, I would appreciate a short review on your preferred site. If you don't do reviews, tell a friend. It really does help. Thank you.

If you would like to hear more about Bad Penny, and keep up with my other work, you can subscribe to the newsletter at joshgentry.co m/newsletter.

979-8-9894799-1-7

Snack Reads Press

www.snackreadspress.com

Cover design by Jennifer Drummond

Cover art created with Midjourney by Josh Gentry, modified by Jennifer Drummond

For Jae, without whom I would accomplish very little,
and for Suzy – catch you next time around

CONTENTS

1. Bad Penny   1

2. Bad Penny   7

3. Donna   13

4. Dark Violet   21

5. Tom   29

6. Bad Penny   32

7. Geezer   46

8. Bad Penny   54

9. Vampire Mayor   66

10. Bad Penny   68

11. Dark Violet   108

12. Bad Penny   111

13. Bad Penny   114

14. Donna   118

15. Tom   122

16. Bad Penny   132

17. Donna   139

18. Bad Penny   142

19.	Donna	145
20.	Bad Penny	150
21.	Tom	154
22.	Geezer	158
23.	Bad Penny	161
Afterword		172
Acknowledgements		173
About the Author		175

1

BAD PENNY

The alley is dark and wet, carpeted with damp trash. The muted illumination of a streetlight turns puddles into silver-edged pools of darkness. I shiver, but not from the cold. I check my equipment again: aluminum vial with stopper, insulated lunch bag, needle and tubing, scalpel, syringe, specimen bags, and antiseptic wipes. No bone saw tonight. I slide the leather doctor's bag behind the dumpster, except for the vial.

The glowing face of my watch tells me it is now or never. Dawn is an hour away, and in the month I have been watching him, he has never cut it this close. I remove the stopper from the vial and down the oily liquid inside in one long swallow. My heart beats faster and my hands tremble slightly as I set the vial down in a puddle. Waiting.

The scar on my inner thigh begins to itch. He is at the mouth of the alley, sliding silently into it. I begin my wounded-bird dance, staggering up against the wall of the alley, leaning my hot forehead against the cool brick. The dance that will bring us together, predator and prey. With a rush as of wings, he is at my side. Easy, this one.

"Lost our way, have we?"

He brushes my hair back from the side of my face. My forehead is still against the brick.

"Aren't you a pretty one."

And he is on me, flinging me around so my back is against the wall. One arm snakes around my waist, lifting me and crushing me against him. I arch my back, bouncing my head off the brick wall. He strikes, his fangs burying themselves in my throat, tapping into the jugular. He is for the fast and furious feast.

My skin catches like wildfire, pouring my heat into his cold, hard body. Waves of pleasure hold me in one long, rigid convulsion against him. I sense him feasting on my ecstasy and fear, as much as my blood. My heart feels like it is beating its way out of my body, then it begins to slow. Slower and slower ... slower, I'm getting cold. He lets me slide to the asphalt. Darkness ...

The pacemaker startles my heart into life. I am on the asphalt, freezing. There was something I was supposed to do. My thoughts are fat, sluggish worms. What was it? What was it, Penny? The bag. I try to crawl. So heavy. I slide forward on my belly, slithering over the vampire's corpse. Finally, my hand finds the smooth, supple leather. I haul myself to my knees and drag the bag from behind the dumpster. The tearing sound of the zipper almost breaks my eardrums.

I fumble within the insulated lunch container, pull the plastic bag out, complete with hook, and hang it from the edge of the dumpster. I pull open my shirt and connect the tubing to the port in my chest. As the transfusion begins, I am shaking violently, a dry, brittle bunch of twigs. When the transfusion is done, I will harvest samples for the Good Doctor, and then go home to sleep. Today is a miracle.

***

It is raining when I wake. Raindrops slide down the window, more beautiful than diamonds, and worthless. I go to the refrigerator, get out the orange juice, and drink two tall glasses. It helps, but not enough. I'm as empty as a discarded plastic bag.

I had rinsed off when I got back from the hit, but now I shower to clear this fog from my brain. Drops slide down my skin, entrancing me. I realize the water is off, but I do not know how long I've been standing here. Sliding my fingers over the scars on my right inner thigh, I shiver.

In front of the mirror I pull a comb haltingly through my hair. This one preferred blonds, so I'm a blond. I've tried wigs, but I'm always afraid they will come off during the action. Scabs are already forming on the two puncture wounds in my neck.

From my closet I select one of my high neck blouses. It's a Victorian style, white blouse with a high, starched collar that covers my entire neck. There is lace around the collar and down the front, and puffy, ornamental sleeves. One twist on tradition, except for the collar and sleeves, its sheer. I wear it over a black bra, and pair it with a short, black skirt. The skirt is snug at the waist but flairs out, emphasizing the slimness of my legs. I pile my long hair into a messy mound, and my fancy trampy look is complete. The shoes are sensible and black. I spend too much time on my feet.

Before leaving the apartment, I pull on a light jacket, so as to attract less attention until I'm at work. I take the insulated lunch container from the fridge. I'll eat when I get to work, but I'm debating grabbing coffee on the way. Time to go out into the world. Today is a miracle.

***

I get off the elevated train in the old industrial district just South of Downtown. There are a few scruffy characters waiting on the platform, but I'm the only rider who gets off. My steps echo on the metal stairs. Don't rush, Penny, but look lively, head up and alert. Happily the Good Doctor's place is within a block of the stop.

The damp is starting to make my clothes feel heavy, but the rain has stopped. I press the plastic button beside a featureless steel door; 1 long, 3 short, 1 long, repeat. I wait, shifting the insulated lunch bag from hand to hand. Sometimes it takes awhile, depending on if she's in the middle of an experiment, or whatever it is she does in there. Come on, I need to get to the bar and make some tips.

The door opens, but no one is there. Every time I look for the mechanism that opens it, but I never spot it. As I walk down the tunnel-like hallway, I can feel the moisture being sucked from my waterlogged clothes and skin. Always dry in here. Doc must have a serious dehumidifier. The temperature never varies, either, no matter what time of year.

At the end of the hallway, I push through a curtain of heavy plastic strips, like they use for walk-in freezers. This is the cramped anteroom where all our interactions take place, except for the surgeries. It contains two armchairs with the stuffing busting through the seems, a tiny side table, and a fluorescent shop light overhead. The door is like a bank vault. After slapping the palm-size button next to it, I sit, crossing my legs and observing with clinical interest how far my skirt slides up my thighs.

Breathing the strange, conditioned air, I remember our initial interview and shiver. That is all behind us. We have a stable, working relationship. She should have no problem with my small request.

The mechanical thud of the lock disengaging is followed by the soundless swinging open of the heavy door. The Good Doctor regards me as if I am an insect she is about to stick a pin through. She closes the door behind her.

I motion to the insulated lunch bag on the side table. I do not hand it to her, because our hands might touch. She picks it up, then takes an aluminum tube from the pocket of her lab coat and sets it carefully on the table. Then she turns back towards the vault door.

"Aren't you going to ask me any details? Height, weight, mottling, lividity?"

"No. I can tell what I need from the samples, now." She starts to turn the dial on the vault. I sit forward on the edge of my chair.

"Wait. There is something I need to ask you."

"For." She pauses. "Something you need to ask me for, yes?"

"Yes." She turns.

"I've been thinking, what happens if they don't drink enough? What if they decide to play with me before they have swallowed a fatal dose?"

She shrugs. "Make sure they are excited enough that they don't. That's procedure."

"I want a second dose, injectable, that I can use as backup."

She eyes me.

"Planning extra kills that you don't have to share with me?"

"No. I want a second dose in a syringe as backup."

She shakes her head. "It is expensive. I do not need you wasting it."

"I'm not going to waste it. I'm going to carry it as a backup in case the first bite fails."

"That's not part of my plan."

"Then this is your last sample."

The temperature in the room drops when smiles. She raises a finger.

"One, you won't quit. Your need to be bitten is too great." She raises a second finger. "Two, I have gleaned perhaps all I can from these small samples. I don't need them any longer."

"You've learned everything? There is always more to know, isn't there? New mysteries?"

"A functional specimen would be most helpful."

"Functional?" I ask.

"Living doesn't seem the right term, in this case."

"Living?" I whistle. "You want a live vamp?"

She licks her lips. "Bring me a live vamp, as you say, and I will give you a second dose."

"You're nuts. I have to die and come back from the dead to kill one, and that is the easy option. Capture and transport a live vamp? Not to mention how long would you last once I got it here? Ixna on that."

Her mouth is a thin line. "Then that is your final dose. Get out."

As I walk back down the hallway, my hands shake and my mouth is dry. Penny, we have a problem.

2

BAD PENNY

"Don't panic, Penny. She didn't mean it. She was just scaring you out of asking for an extra dose." My hands shake and my mouth is dry, as I walk from the train stop to work. I can't stop being bitten. I have tried, I can't, but keep getting bitten and eventually a vamp is going to kill you. With the Good Doctor's program, I have a measure of control, a shot at survival. If she takes that away, I will not live another year.

Right now, though, I have to pull it together and pay the rent. I turn down the alley before I reach the front entrance to The Night Fowl. As I approach the back door, a bum stirs next to the dumpster, causing a rustling of cardboard boxes and old newspapers. Bright eyes peer out through the tangle of greasy, salt-and-pepper hair and beard.

"Hello, Little Bird," he says, with a throat that has had sandpaper taken to it.

"Hey, John. How are they hanging?"

"Low, loose and full of juice. Will the Little Bird bring John a fat, juicy worm?"

"No promises."

He smiles a small, strange smile. As the door closes behind me, I hear him mutter, "Never from you, Little Bird."

The kitchen I enter is greasy and hot. By the time I punch my time card and leave through the swinging doors at the other end of the kitchen, I won't be able to shake the feeling that I have acquired a thin coating. There aren't many roaches, though, and I have never seen a rat in here. Rob, the owner, looks up from his desk in the corner, his bald head sweating.

"You're late again, " he snarls.

I ignore him.

"You're attitude stinks, Penny."

"I've heard that. I listen to self-help book after self-help book while I sleep. Nothing seems to take."

"You think you can show up any time you want, is that it?"

I shove my card into the time clock. Punch.

"We talked about this. I've got latitude."

"Come over here and I'll show you some latitude," he mutters, already looking back down at his paperwork, a verbal tick. He probably doesn't know he said it. If I recorded it and played it back to him, he would look at me puzzled, and then with growing alarm, as if I might be from a parallel universe like in that shitty SciFi show his girlfriend makes him watch. Truth is, I have too many regulars for him to fire me. Too many customers who would stop coming if I wasn't here.

"Hey," he, says, surprising me because I thought he was done. "You being careful walking here alone? You know, with all the ... dangers and stuff out there?"

He doesn't look directly at me. No one wants to be direct about those dangers in the night, like talking about them might draw them to you. Still, it's sweet of him to ask.

"Come on, Rob, you know I'm the scariest bitch around."

I exit the kitchen through the swinging double doors. Except for the kitchen, the Night Fowl is one long, low room. Mismatched, battered furniture, all dark, is scattered about. In one dim corner, some old pallets with plywood over the top serve as a stage. There's a grimy film of desperation on the tables and the patrons alike.

Scanning my section, I spot several regulars, waiting. Good. I need groceries, and the rent is due in a week. Francis sees me and raises a hand to wave, an uncertain smile lighting his face. Angela spots me at the same time and high-speed sashays towards me. I look to the bar. Ned, the barkeep, nods at me. I head his way. Angela intercepts, blocking me.

"I've been covering your section for an hour," she whines.

"You're an angel," I reply.

"Screw you."

I smile sweetly. "How's tips?"

"Penny's Irregulars won't even order until you get here. You know that."

"Sounds like hard work." I move to step around her. She moves with me.

"It won't last forever, you know. Your little empire."

"Good luck storming the gates."

I step around her and move to the bar. Ned has two drinks ready on a tray, and three more empty glasses waiting. He understands where the tips come from, and he's good at his job. As I approach, he points at the tray.

"Rum and cola for Francis, Bourbon up for Tom."

I smile at him as I pick up the tray. Tips will do the rest of the thanking. I head for Francis's table. Pulling out the chair across from him, I sit, no smile.

"Hi, Fran. Here's your drink."

Francis is typical of my regulars. Practically forty, wife and kid at home, dead-end job that pays the bills, barely. Not a bad sort, but straying into dangerous waters.

"How've you been, Penny?"

"Suitable for daily use, if your standards aren't too high."

He looks down into his drink.

"Um, I bet, yeah." He takes a gulp of his Rum and cola.

"How did your daughter's recital go?"

He looks up, a genuine smile lighting his face.

"Really well. She's really good." He starts rocking gently forward and backward in his chair. "You can be having a shitty day and just listening to her play makes all the ugly fade away." He stops rocking and looks down into his drink again. "I just wish she'd talk to me once in a while. We used to be really close, you know?" Like I've been a family friend for years. He takes another gulp.

I lean across the table and put my hand on his forearm. Looking him in the eye, I squeeze his arm hard, for a three count. Then I stand up and move on.

Tom is a car salesman, with a fake tan and disturbingly white teeth. Someone has to sell cars, I guess, and someone has to serve them drinks. As I approach, he slides his chair back from the table and slaps his thighs.

"Have a seat, Babe."

I pull out the chair across from him and sit, no smile.

"Here's your drink, Tom."

"That's never going to work, is it?" he asks.

"Never know unless you try."

He slides back up to the table.

"That's what I like about you, Penny. You aren't some thin-skinned, uppity bitch who can't take a compliment."

"I thought it was my ass you liked."

His white teeth flash.

"That, too. Hey, how about you let me take you someplace nice on your evening off. I can get a Mercedes, Caddy, anything you want. We'll go out on the town in style."

I stand.

"Enjoy the view." I turn and walk away, making eye contact with my next patron. He is new. I can tell by his eyes that he is already lost.

If you had to guess my age, you'd guess anywhere from 15 to 25. I am 29. I could be your daughter or your paramour. My slim body and big eyes say girl, but the way I look through your facade says anything but innocent. My vulnerability makes you want to protect me, from every monster but yourself. I'm a little girl with a wicked streak, and a woman worn down by the sordidness of life. I bring out your best, and your worst. You are doomed.

They ask me to meet them, in parked cars and expensive hotel rooms. They would pay, most of them. I never go. Except when I do, but never for money. I understand the Need. I am not without compassion.

Shift over, I exit the back door of the Night Fowl into the alley. Shadows shift, and a large, indistinct form looms silently out of the darkness. "Have you got that juicy worm, Little Bird?"

Extending my arm, I dangle a paper bag with grease beginning to soak through.

"A good night," I say. "Cook had to remake two orders."

It is always surprising when something that big moves that fast. Silent as some back alley owl, he swoops into the pool of illumination thrown by the light over the door, snatches the bag from my hand, and soars back into the night. A whispered, "Thank you," traces his path back to where I stand. I shiver. Even a greasy bum can be mysterious when you are in the city's nocturnal embrace.

I put one foot in front of the other.

3

DONNA

Donna used to look forward to the last day of the month. Reports due, payroll to be verified, bills to mail, wrapping up four weeks of work and putting a bow on it. She even used to tidy up her desk and use furniture polish on it, that citrus smell better than any man's cologne. Thirty years will take the shine off just about anything, she guesses. God knows none of her marriages lasted that long. Two more last days of the month and its retirement on that fat City Hall pension, the one she'd her eye on even as a graduate of Miss Rhoda's Clerical School for Girls.

"Everybody got to work, but you work for the Government and you can retire while you still got some life in you," her Momma had told her. She hopes Momma was right.

In walks one of the reasons this job has taken on a funky smell. He has to turn sideways to go through the door, he's so wide, thus his nickname, the Wall. Biggest man she ever damn seen. He's got that stupid smirk on his face, like always.

"Morning, Nonnina. Your lucky morning. The Wall is here."

"Smelled you coming. Sack of shit carries."

He throws back his head and roars, the way he does every month. He doesn't smell like shit, he smells like cheap suits and money. If she could bottle it she would name it, Inevitability, and sell it outside every town hall on the planet. She points to the envelope in her outbox.

"The check is ready, Mr. Wall. I wouldn't want to keep an important man like yourself. Good day."

He picks up the envelope with a huge, pink hand and slips it into the inside pocket of his white sports coat, then drops a twenty on her desk.

"Lunch is on me, Nonnina. You should have a drink, and toast the Wall, huh."

She waits until he leaves to smooth out the bill and add it to the others in the fat envelope in the bottom drawer of the desk. Momma didn't raise no crooks, but she didn't raise no fools, neither. "Remember, ain't no one playin fair," Momma had told her. Ain't no one playin fair.

***

Donna locks the door to the Mayor's office behind her at exactly 3 PM. Any citizens who have business with the Mayor but don't have his direct number will have to wait until tomorrow. Riding the elevator down with fleeing city employees from the other floors, she is already anticipating getting home and slipping her feet into house shoes. Her oldest is always chiding her to take the stairs to get exercise. Her oldest doesn't wear heels.

She congregates at the bus stop with the other professionals, a few tourists staring up at the skyscrapers, and a couple homeless. She recognizes two of them, one a man wearing a yamaka and a good but old-fashioned suit. He always smiles at her, and she thinks him handsome. The other is a woman in the same kind of bland office wear that is Donna's uniform, and who uses a silver-handled cane. Donna nods to both, but they don't speak. She has only ever had one bus stop friend, a woman who worked as a cleaning lady in the bank building on the corner. Donna had found it annoying, at first, when the other woman insisted on chatting away at her, but it turned out they had children the same age, and had grown up just a few blocks from each other, although they couldn't remember ever meeting as children.

"You got to have woman friends your own age," Momma always said. "That's where you get help when you need it." Grace had been there for her when Donna was sick and the kids needed watching, and Donna had helped care for Grace's mother before she went to the old folks' home. Donna stiffened at the thought of the city-run home. Those had been different times.

Donna isn't sure why she is thinking about Grace today, but by the time the bus drops her off and she is walking down her street, she is feeling a bit melancholy. The street bustles, oblivious to her mood. Teenagers congregate on the corner, knots of boys and girls on opposite sides of the street, taunting each other. Old folks without much to do sit on the front steps of row houses, talking about the old days, or watching life stream by.

Over the years, people have tried to differentiate the marching lines of brick buildings on each side of the street. Few of the houses are painted the same color as their immediate neighbors. Variations of red, brown and yellow are the most popular, but the occasional pink or green makes a statement. In recent years, those that can afford it have started replacing the beautiful, leaky old windows with ugly modern ones that do a better job of keeping out the cold. Donna can't bring herself to do that, although, in January, she understands those who do.

Donna nods to neighbors on her side of the street as she passes them, the genuineness of her smile varying depending on who it is. As she starts up the steps of her own flower pot festooned stoop, Mrs. Beardsley, her neighbor directly to the North, bursts out through her screen door.

"Your tenants were blaring that noise they call music on Sunday morning again, Donna. You know that's not right."

Donna shrugged. "It's the poetry of our youth, Velma. They got to express themselves."

Mrs. Beardsley snorted. "They can damn well wait until after noon on the Lord's day to poeticize about their ho's."

Donna sighs and nods tiredly. "I'll talk to them again, Velma. You know kids."

"I do, Lord help us all. You have a good evenin', Donna."

"You, too, Velma."

Velma has been her neighbor for twenty years. They are in one of their friendly phases, but those boys upstairs are going to test it, no doubt. Of course, her youngest, Janelle, is also a culprit when it comes to the music, but Velma didn't need to know that.

The front door isn't locked, because between her three girls, and the two boys living upstairs, someone was always home. As soon as she closes the door behind her, she kicks off her heels and slips her feet into the house shoes waiting by the door. Alison, her oldest, steps half out of the kitchen and waves at her.

"Welcome home, Momma. Come on into the kitchen. Early dinner tonight. Janelle has class."

Donna gives one long look of longing at her TV in the sitting room, where her shows would be recorded for her. Janelle is getting an education, putting herself through night school with a little help from everyone in the family. Wouldn't be right to make her late for class. Donna sighs and heads for the kitchen.

Allison has a baby on one hip and is cooking with the other hand. Her husband is a fireman, and his job keeps him at the station overnight sometimes. Allison hates being alone, and she and the baby stay with Donna and Janelle on those nights. Donna didn't mind because she didn't have to cook those nights.

"Have a seat, Momma. It's leftovers night, so it's easy. Almost done heating everything up."

"You stop telling me what to do and hand over my Grandbaby."

"Serves me right for trying to be nice," but Allison gives her a little smile of thanks as she shifts so Donna can take the baby. Allison tries a little too hard to take care of everyone, doesn't keep much back for herself. Donna tries not to take advantage, but it can be hard. She has barely sat down when she hears the front door open, then shut again. She knows it is Ida by her footsteps, slow, almost languorous. Her middle daughter stops in the doorway to the kitchen and leans against the door frame.

"I'm here," she says quietly, her smile always with a little devil showing through. She got that from her Daddy.

"Well hallelujah, now everything's going to be alright," Allison mutters, not looking up from the stove.

Ida winks at Donna, then comes and sits beside her at the table.

"Why is dinner so early?" Ida asks.

"Janelle had to reschedule her lab time because of her lab partner's schedule," Allison answers.

"God, you'd think the world revolved around that girl."

Allison turns from the stove, spatula in hand, frowning. "You know how important ...", but sees the mischief in Ida's eyes, and stops, almost smiling. She shakes her head and turns back to the stove. Donna looks at Ida.

"Your Sister might want some help."

"I doubt it," Ida drawls.

"No thank you."

Donna just shakes her head and coos at the baby.

They feel the vibration of Janelle running across the old hardwood floor before she bounces into the kitchen, sliding the straps of her backpack over her shoulders as she goes. She heads straight to the fridge, grabs a can of diet soda, and slams the door shut, the contents rattling. Donna winces.

"Hi, Momma. Hi, Ida. Bye Momma. Bye Allison."

"Just where do you think you're going without eating your supper?" Allison asks.

"You know I have school," Janelle barked back.

"Which is why we are eating early. It's fifteen minutes before you told me you had to go. Sit down and eat. You know what Momma says."

"An empty stomach makes for an empty head," Allison and Ida recite in unison, Ida almost singing it. Janelle turns to Donna.

"Momma, tell them I can't become an Engineer sitting around the table gossiping."

"Maybe you should reconsider your profession," Ida taunts gently.

"Oh, what, and be a camgirl slut like you?" asks Janelle.

"It does make for flexible hours, but no, Honey, you don't have the … personality for it," Ida answers.

"Sit down eat something. Your sisters are right," Donna says.

"Don't sit down yet," Allison says. "Grab the drinks from the fridge."

Janelle drops her backpack by her chair and stalks over to the refrigerator in a huff. She pulls out a plastic pitcher filled with candy red liquid.

"I know Momma wants church punch. What do you two want?"

"Diet soda for me, please," Ida says.

"Me, too," responds Allison.

As Janelle puts the cans on the table and pours punch for Donna and herself, Allison starts putting dishes on the table.

"It's leftovers buffet. Help yourselves."

When they are all seated, they bow their heads, and Allison says, "Dear Lord, Thank you for this bounty. Amen."

Donna serves herself first. Once she has slid a big piece of lasagna onto her plate, hands start crisscrossing the table.

"This catfish I brought home from work is good," Janelle says, taking one of the fillets. "Especially with hot sauce. Someone else can have the collard greens, though." She scrunched up her face.

Allison takes the other piece of catfish. Ida dumps the collard greens onto her plate, next to the lo mein from Noodle Palace. Donna eyes Ida's plate.

"You always did like the strangest combinations," Donna says.

Allison chuckles. "You remember when all she would eat for breakfast was those cheese puffs omelets she was making."

Janelle covers her mouth. "Oh my God that was disgusting."

Donna laughs. In her mind's eye, she sees an excited twelve-year-old Ida serving up her monstrous creation, so proud of herself.

Ida puts on her most regal air, "Early signs of my propensity for adventure," then laughs along with the others.

For the next few minutes they chatted amiably about how things are at Allison's husband's fire station, and which of Janelle's professors at the night school are worthless. Ida and Janelle discuss the specifications of a new camera Ida is buying. There is a lull in conversation as the four women are taking their last bites.

Donna suddenly remembers something.

"Ida, you did pick up my dress from the cleaners like I asked?"

"Yes, Momma, but I forgot to bring it in. I'll go get it out of the car."

"Wait till you're done eating."

"Another late-night meeting, Momma? This mayor is a slave driver," says Allison.

Donna looks around the table at her three babies, then down at her plate.

"You have no idea, honey. You have no idea."

4

——— • ———

Dark Violet

Dark Violet tap, tap, taps her fingernails on the tabletop and looks around the room to see if she's succeeding at annoying the prey. The woman from the human Mayor's office meets her eyes, not in challenge, more like weary acknowledgment. She looks distinguished, white pantsuit flattering salt-and-pepper hair and contrasting with her dark skin, but Violet knows she's just a secretary. She is brave, though. The rest of the City government cowards send her by herself. Before the Covenant, Violet would've had her for a snack while waiting. Like eight-year-old Scotch the secretary would be, mellowed some by time, but still with plenty of vim and vigor. Violet is tapping in time with her heart. Covenant or no, Violet is going to drain that one, one day.

Not so the dowdy middle-aged woman in tweed, next to the secretary. Underboss to the Don or not, these nails tapping on the table will rip her throat one day, she and her monstrosity of a son. The pretty boy seated with them reaches over and puts his hand on top of Violet's. It is like a live wire has been dropped on her skin.

"Please, Mistress, you know I have sensitive ears." After staring into his eyes with excruciating longing, she leans back in her chair. He holds himself with the elegant posture she taught him when he was part of her menagerie, before he was ripped from her and exchanged for that Quisling Gangster. His chair, next to her, is empty. Irresponsible as ever. Sitting in chairs along the wall, are the rest of her Mayor's administration.

The Vampire Mayor, her Lord, enters at ten minutes after the hour, as he always does, pathetic power play. He is dressed like a fucking peasant, with sloppy, ill-fitting clothes and ugly boots of the kind worn by laborers. It is a travesty to bend the knee to such a crude beast. For all that, when his eyes have traveled the table and settled on her, she shivers. His eyes are razor blades.

"Where is your charge, Dark Violet?"

"I do not track the whereabouts of that piece of ..." He raises a warning eyebrow. She turns to the Mob representatives and smiles. "... that fine example of manhood." A certain amount of tension drains from them now that they won't have to defend their Gangster with fangs. Not that they love him more than she does. A pleasant thought occurs to her.

"Perhaps the mysterious hunter has taken him."

This brings a rare frown to the Vampire Mayor's face.

"Don't spread stupid rumors, Violet. There is no mysterious hunter, no bogeyman in the night, except for us." That last bit seems to cheer him up. He smiles benignly at her.

The dowdy mobstress speaks up. "We've also noticed more vampire disappearances than usual. I don't think you should blow it off completely."

"Why would you care if someone is hunting our kind?" Violet asks. "You hate us."

"That's enough, Violet."

His growl causes her to freeze for a moment.

"No one here hates our partners."

The mobstress holds out her small, pudgy hands in a gesture that takes in the whole room. "The Covenant's good for business, good for all of us. It screws with all of us if the balance is threatened."

Violet's Lord addresses her again. "Do you have any proof of this supposed Vampire hunter?"

"Nothing concrete to tie him to specific disappearances, but we suspect the Preacher."

He shakes his head. "No. He knows that we leave his flock alone, and that we would slaughter them all if he interfered with us."

"Again, you mean. If he interfered with us, again." He frowns at her for the second time, and she thinks she might be pushing her luck. As she is wont to do.

"It's not him. It's not anyone." He shifts in his chair, indicating the topic is closed. "Donna, please read the minutes from the last meeting."

***

Violet struggles not to rip the doors off their hinges and set the building on fire, as she leaves the meeting. That pathetic twat, laboring to reduce vampirism from its glorious monstrousness to the mundaneness of a trade union. Once a peasant, always a peasant. She spits on the floor as she crosses the threshold of the building into the voluptuous night.

A walk through the nighttime city, her city, always helps restore her sangfroid after one of the Vampire Mayor's infuriating meetings. She moves soundlessly through the empty streets. This had once been the Vampire District, apparently abandoned warehouses containing palaces and dark, blood-soaked dungeons. The street had teemed with people and monsters then, her senses almost overwhelmed by the bright sounds of merry-making and murder, the thick smells of love and slaughter. God it had been good. But then the war had begun, the human vermin led by zealots who could not be bribed or cowed. Richard had ridden that tide of chaos up from the docks, or the gutter, or wherever he came from, and seized power before the vampire aristocrats, like Violet, knew what was happening. He made peace with the humans and became the first Vampire Mayor. How had they let it happen? How had she let it happen?

It takes several city blocks to put behind her the joyless domain of the Vampire Mayor. She begins to see, and smell, people on the street. People that you see at night, with long hair or shaved heads, tattooed and pierced people, dressed to impress their own kind in boots and stockings, leather and lace. Another block or two and the type of people on the street shifts. Mixed among the night people, she begins to see college students in blue jeans and hoodies or tight dresses in bright colors. Sprinkled in were refugees from the suburbs, in blazers and little black dresses, sometimes with a spray of gray in their hair, and the beginnings of a paunch. These were sometimes more desperate and reckless than the young.

It was here, on the border between the old vampire district and the still bustling downtown, that Violet turned off the street and floated down grimy steps to a blank, steel door. In response to her knock, a slot opened at eye level, allowing dim light to leach out into the cement stairwell. She gave the watcher behind the door her full grin, fangs displayed.

The door opened and she breezed through, lightly patting Jeffrey on the arm in greeting. She was in a dim corridor that ended in another door about twenty feet further on.

"How is the crowd tonight?" she tossed back over her shoulder. She got the usual grunt in reply, which made her laugh. Jeffrey would prefer the guests to sit and quietly drink themselves to death, so he was always grumpy. A few rare, growled words reached her down the hall.

"The car salesman is here."

She clapped her hands twice and giggled. It was no end of fun tormenting the smarmy, ridiculous human. That he was useful to her was icing on the cake. The clamor quieted momentarily on her entrance but roared back even louder as she was recognized. Employees smiled at her deferentially. Guests shouted and waved their invitations for her to join them. She stood and took it in, shaking off the last of the anger and frustration from the Vampire Mayor's meeting.

The establishment was a long, narrow room. A huge, dark mahogany bar dominated the left-hand side. Smartly dressed bar tenders, in suspenders and bow ties regardless of gender, served up cocktails such as virgin's blood with coriander and orange peel, or transfusion of dock worker injected with nitrogen and anise. Violet herself had created the Sundown, blood of leukemia patient poured over black cherry syrup. What you would not find was any senior citizen or street person blood. She was running a class establishment.

Tiny tables were crammed into the right-hand side of the room, an impossibly narrow aisle separating them from the bar. Larger parties and VIPs occupied the few booths along the wall. At the far end, the little stage is empty now, but later Danil and Sandra would do a selection of the great love scenes from the plays of Krakowski, the greatest of the vampire writers.

There is nowhere in North America, now, that you can see a full Krakowski play performed, with a truly professional cast and the elegant stage production that the dramas deserved. She'd spent last Winter in the warm arms of Brazil and Argentina, and there she had experienced the great works as never before, the purity of the poet's vision imbued with a Latin sensuality that, to her surprise and delight, transmuted it into something even more. Humans in the audience had to be restrained from throwing themselves on stage, begging to be the final meal shared by Christopher and Ana, the night before they were tragically slaughtered by that barbarian, Attila the Hun. She had vowed then to bring Krakowski back to her home. This small stage was only the humble beginning. She'd already commissioned the architect of the theater in Sao Paulo to design for her the most beautiful theater this city had ever seen.

Right this moment is not the time for the sublime, however. Now is the time to see what the sleazy little man waiting in the kitchen has for her. She glides behind the bar and soundlessly through the swinging door into the kitchen. She prefers stealth because she is a predator, but also because you catch people being their real selves.

He is standing very near one of the special orders. The woman lies prone and unmoving on the rolling table. From ankles to neck her body is covered in food, and it is clear that is all she is covered by. A blindfold covers her eyes, and her wrists and ankles are tied to the table. Violet's menu is divided in two, the Willing and the Unwilling. She knows this item is from the willing side, but he has no way of knowing that. Even the willing are given a mild sedative to prevent them from squirming too early and ruining their presentation.

The man with the fake tan and vulgar suit tentatively reaches out a hand, trembling.

"Have some," she says quietly.

He jerks his hand away and spins towards her. She chuckles and waves a hand dismissively. "There's plenty of time to cover up what we take, as long as we aren't too greedy." She plucks a cherry off one of the girl's breasts and keeps her eyes on his face as she bends and licks the nipple it has hidden. Such emotions war within him. She sees hunger, lust, but also revulsion at her, but mostly for himself. This is why he amuses her, always in such agony. She stands up straight and meets his gaze with hers.

"You're loss," she says, making her voice a caress. Then faster than he can see coming, she reaches across the meal and slaps him, sending him reeling backwards, crashing into more of the rolling tables. Violet laughs gaily.

"What the fuck did you do that for?" He raises his hand to his mouth, touching the trickle of gorgeous red at the corner. Her throat tightens. She has to be so careful or she will eat all the useful humans.

"It's because I like you, Thomas. You know I like you. It's my way of showing affection."

"More like playing with the mouse," he mutters. "And only my Mother calls me Thomas."

She bares her fangs in her full grin. "Then it must be very strange coming from me."

He pales but does not look away. She respects that about him, that he doesn't look away from things.

"What information did you bring me, Thomas?"

"I, uh, I got a call. Supposed to have a car ready tomorrow tonight for a certain toothy gangster."

"Don't they have their own fleet of cars? Why wouldn't he take one of them?"

He shrugs. "We sold them most of those cars, so I know they have some extra features, like the ability to track their location."

"You think he's hiding something from them. Interesting. Any idea what?"

"Nah. Likely as not he just wants some privacy to meet up with some tail."

She snorts. "Maybe that's what you'd do if you were an immortal crime lord, but we probably shouldn't judge based on you."

He shrugs, again. "I've done my bit."

"So you have." She goes to a desk in the back corner of the kitchen and retrieves a hundred-dollar bill from one of the drawers. She meant to tease him when she gave it to him, but she can see he has had enough for today. He practically snatches it from her fingers, and slinks out the back, into the alley.

5

Tom

Tom does the crossword to occupy his mind, trying to keep from getting the jitters. Most of the lights are off in the dealership. It's after hours and the sun has just gone down. Some lucrative business is about to happen, which normally makes him as happy as a Freshman football player about to meet the cheerleaders for the first time, but he doesn't care for the bloodsuckers. The gangsters he is fine with. He knows how to act with them, the right mix of ass-kissing and wink-wink-nudge-nudge. But the bloodsuckers, well they aren't human, are they? How do you schmooze that shit?

And this one, he's both, which is worse. Gangster turned vamp so he can be some kind of ambassador of creepy. Tom isn't supposed to know that, but gangsters gossip like housewives at book club. They are creeped out by the Vamp Capo too, but they don't have any choice about working for it. The powers-that-be formed the Covenant a few years ago, and all the little people have to dance to the new tune.

Creepy as it is, some say it's better this way. The competition between the vamps and the gangsters got bad. Between them and the cops militarizing up to try and get control of the streets back, the city had been on the verge of becoming a full-blown war zone. A nobody like Tom could get caught in that crossfire. Now everybody has their own turf, knows their place. It's a hell of a lot safer, or so people tell themselves.

The chime goes off which means a car drove into the lot. All you have to do, Tommy, is hand over the keys and take the envelope. Easy-peasy-lemon-squeezy. He screams like a little girl when the hand falls on his shoulder. His legs try to jump him over the counter, but that grip is like an iron clamp. It turns him around to look into flat, dead eyes. What a giant asshole.

"Jesus fucking Mary Magdalene! Why you gotta do that when your boys are driving through the front gate like civilized people?"

Still grinding the bones of his shoulder together with one hand, the Vamp Capo holds out the other. Tom gets the keys from his pocket and drops them into his hand. "Range Rover, as requested. You know you ever want something with a little more class, we got Caddy's, we got vintage, too. I got a sweet little Jaguar ..."

"Stop talking."

"Yeah, I get that a lot, occupational hazard."

The vampire squeezes harder. Tom bites his tongue to keep from whimpering.

"The boys have your money. I'm ditching them tonight. They'll be pissed, but a lone hunter has to hunt alone." It pauses for a moment like it is trying to remember something, then it winks at Tom. If Tom could crawl out of his own skin to get away from it, he would. It lets go of his shoulder, stuffs a bill in the pocket of his sports coat, and then it is gone.

Tom pulls a comb from his pocket and runs it through his hair once, twice, three times. The tough boys will be coming through the door any second and they'll be relieved their boss is already gone, but also scarred because they're supposed to keep an eye on it. He'll calm their nerves with a little patter, get the money, and then it's going to be time for a drink.

6

— · —

BAD PENNY

I put a double shot of tequila and a slice of lime in front of Sergio. He stares down my shirt while I am leaning over the table.

"I like the new bra, Chica," he says. "A little lace is always classy. Makes a man feel like he's going upscale. Scoring the good stuff." He winks.

Sergio is alright. A little rough around the edges, but I don't think there is a mean bone in his body. Unless he's drunk, then steer clear, which is why I cut him off after two tequilas. He doesn't mind, knows it's for his own good. He keeps his hands to himself, except when he sometimes hugs me goodnight. I know he is sad if he hugs me. I don't mind at all.

"I like being on this end when she leans over a table," says Tom from the table behind me. He's one I have come close to breaking his fingers for him.

"Men are pigs," says Nicky, in her best whiskey and cigarettes voice. Nicky, who we used to call Nick. She is on my left.

Tom snorts. "You should know, Toots. Like your hand didn't accidentally brush my leg as I walked by."

I look at Nicky and raise an eyebrow. She laughs, uncrossing and crossing her long, muscular legs.

"Girl's gotta have some fun in this shit hole."

Sergio chuckles and downs half his tequila.

"Careful," Tom says. "You're going to hurt Penny's feelings. This is your second home, isn't it, Penny? If you have a home. It's a mythical destination, like Shangra-La." He leers at me.

"Keep dreaming, Prester John," I reply.

"Francis claims to have been to the mountain top. I'll get it out of the little turd eventually."

"He's more afraid of her than you," snorts Donna from my right. She is a thick, middle-aged woman who dresses in respectable office-ware but still somehow fits in here.

"What, she's going to break his legs?"

"No," Donna says, looking at me with laughing eyes. "Stop talking to him."

Tom starts to make another asinine comment, but something catches his eye by the door and he turns pale under his fake tan. He looks down at his drink and says low and urgent, "Penny, sit down at Sergio's table. Face away from the door. Don't look around."

I do it. Sergio looks confused, then he focuses on something behind me and his eyes go wide.

"Dios mío!."

There is a sharp intake of breath from either Nicky or Donna. From behind me comes the clatter and scrape of chairs overturning and tables sliding. I look at Tom. Staring into his drink he says, "The Wall."

Nodding, I look at Sergio.

"How about those Wolverines, huh? Can you believe they lost a ten-point lead in the last two minutes of the game?"

He is still staring.

"Serge, look at me."

He does, then shakes his head. "I don't follow basketball. I'm a baseball man."

A hand the size of a catcher's mitt engulfs my right shoulder, picking me up out of the chair and turning me around like I'm a rag doll. Joey the Wall sets me on my feet, facing him. He is at least seven feet tall and almost as wide. His legs and arms are like tree trunks. Topping it all off is a bald bullet head with mean little eyes.

"Give the Wall a kiss, Babe," he says.

"I have strict rules against making out with architectural elements."

He squeezes and I can feel the bones of my shoulder rub together. My knees start to buckle from the pain, but I catch myself on the table with my other arm.

"That's the smart mouth I've been missing. Still haven't been broken, huh, Penny? Damn, that's gonna be fun."

"For somebody, but not for you, Joey," I say through gritted teeth.

He shakes me a little. "I'm not another lonely drunk for you to milk for tips, Penny. I'm an important man, a leader in the community. Come on, I'll show you."

He shifts his hand to my upper arm and starts to drag me toward the back. His grip says he will break my arm if I don't come along. I want to twist around and knee him in the balls, but he's too damn big to mess with if you don't have to. I try to keep my feet and as much dignity as I can.

Turning my head, I throw a wink over my shoulder and make sure none of Penny's Irregulars are doing anything stupid. Nicky is pulling Sergio back down into his chair. Tom sits with his hands spread on top of the table, staring into his drink.

The Wall turns sideways to fit through the door into the back. He starts towards Rob's desk, but no one is there. Our cook didn't show tonight, so Rob is in the kitchen cooking. I'm not feeling helpful, so

I keep my mouth shut. The Wall stops in the middle of the room and shouts.

"Where are you, you little prick? You're two weeks late on your premium."

"Premium? Really," I ask.

"If I want you to open your mouth, I'll tell you to get on your knees."

I roll my eyes. Rob peeks around the corner of the kitchen. Tilting my head towards the door, I try to signal him to sneak out. He blows it, though. He freezes when he sees Joey. The Wall spots him and growls, pointing at Rob's desk. Rob immediately starts towards it.

"Not with that filthy apron on. Show some respect."

Rob almost trips over himself as he reverses, pulls the apron off over his head, and tosses it into the kitchen. The Wall laughs.

"No wonder I never eat in this roach palace."

"I never had roaches in here. Or rats." Rob shows a flare of anger and a centimeter of backbone. The Wall gets very still.

"You disrespecting me, Rob?" he asks in a quiet voice.

"No .. no, Wall. I wouldn't do that, man."

"Man?"

"Sir. I would never disrespect you, Sir. Just...just let me get your money."

As Rob scurries past, the Wall kicks him in the butt, sending him stumbling the rest of the way to the desk. Rob yelps, but doesn't respond otherwise. I stand as relaxed as I can, to encourage the Wall to relax his grip on my arm. Makes it easier to twist away if I need to, or at least saves some bruises.

Rob pulls a cash box from the bottom drawer of his desk that I didn't know was there. He dials the combination, opens it, and removes a thick envelope. The Wall finally lets go of my arm, walks up to the desk and takes the envelope. His body language changes and his voice gets a little more friendly. Towering over Rob, who is still seated, he says, "Now that you are square, I predict that surprise health inspection tomorrow will go just fine." He turns to me. "See, Penny, I'm a bona fide citizen, greasing the wheels of commerce, helping the small businessman navigate shark-infested waters." He gestures broadly in the direction of Rob.

I snort.

"That's a cop threat. What are you, working for the city? Am I going to see you picking up trash in the parks now? You'd make a great crossing guard. Traffic would stop for you for sure."

His face flushes, and I sense he is genuinely angry for the first time since he walked into the bar.

"You think you're smart, Penny, but you're just clever. You don't know shit about the Covenant. You could be eaten up by this town's machinery and never know why. You're just another ignorant slag with better legs."

He spits out the words, losing control of himself. Then he stops, still breathing rapidly, but calming down. A suspicious light enters his eyes.

"Or maybe you do know something, and you're using it to needle me. You still hanging around that freak the Preacher?"

Ah, that's why he's never tried to force me.

"We're in touch," I reply.

"I bet you are," he leers and suddenly lumbers at me. I step aside and prepare to run, but he barges through the door back into the bar. We can hear his progress towards the exit even back here. Then it is quiet.

Rob mops sweat from his forehead with the back of his hand. We pretend it is from the heat of the kitchen.

"Penny, you might just attract too much attention to be worth it."

"Got his attention off you and your late premium," I say.

He laughs shakily. "OK. You get to play for another day. Now get out there and take care of customers. The Irregulars are no doubt having a hemorrhage.

I put on my best wise-ass smile and walk back through the swinging doors. What the hell is the covenant?

***

Exiting the back door of the Night Fowl into the alley, I do not see John. He's a survivor. He'll find dinner somewhere.

I put one foot in front of the other. Someone told me once that if I counted my footsteps for my whole life, the sum would be the answer to a great mystery, but I'm too easily distracted. I pass one alley, then another, and another, a world perpendicular to this one that tries to suck me in. Just go home, Penny. Then the First Bite, the one on my right inner thigh, begins to itch. There is a Vamp close. Keep moving, don't let it know you know it's there. Now the itching is a burning. Don't show fear. Don't smell like fear. Do not be prey.

He is ahead of me, and he has his arm around a kid, a Goddamn kid. Keep walking, Penny. You are not a superhero. Only engage on your terms, when the trap is set. That is how you survive.

He turns the boy down the next alley. Shit. I wasn't planning to die a heroic death tonight. As I pass, I dart a glance down the alley. He is backing the boy up against the side of the alley, into shadows. The boy is maybe 12 or 13? Short life. What is he doing out here, dammit?

I am passed the alley now. It's an apartment building. Fuck it. I run up the gray concrete steps and hit all the buzzers next to the door as fast as I can, using both hands. There is a buzz and I slam through the door into a dimly lit entryway. Wildly I look for the stairs. They are on my left. I hurl myself up the stairs, 2, 4, 6. I lurch to a halt. One of the wooden spindles in the banister is partly broken. I kick it once, twice, and with the sound of splintering wood, it falls to the floor. I run back down the stairs and grab it. One end is satisfyingly pointed. Heart pounding, I race back to the stairs and up to the first landing. Here's the window that must be the one I saw above the vampire and the boy. Someone has left it part way open to ventilate the stairwell. I set my stake on the floor and slowly raise the window as far as it will go.

Sticking my head out, I look down. They are directly below me. I pull my head back in, pick up the stake, then swing one leg and then the other out the window, sitting on the sill. I lean forward as far as I dare and look down. The vampire should have heard me, but he is enraptured now, leaning over the boy, fangs surely buried in his neck.

With luck I will break the vampire's neck, stunning him long enough to stake him. I'll probably hurt the boy, too, but hopefully not badly. I slide off the sill and plunge towards them, feet first.

The vampire looks up at the last instant. My feet slam into his back and shoulder. "Damn, I missed his head," I have just time to think before crashing to the alley floor on my back, knocking the air from my lungs. The vampire and boy are knocked sprawling. I struggle to a sitting position, trying to get to my feet, but the vampire is already up. Too strong, too fast. His fangs gleam in the dark as he snarls his rage.

Behind him a rubbish pile churns, as a dark form rolls out of it and towards the back of the vampire's legs. The vampire hesitates, beginning to turn its head to look over its shoulder. I leap to my feet screaming, "Liberty or Death, Motherfucker!" at the top of my lungs. His head jerks back to me, eyes wild. At the same time, the form rolls into the back of his legs, and I crash into his chest, sending him over.

Kneeling on top of him, I drive the stake into his chest with both arms and all of my strength. I yank the stake back out and drive it home again, and again and again.

I do not stop until my arms will no longer move. I sit on its prone form, sobbing, covered in its blood. What was its chest is now an unrecognizable mess of bloody meat and bone. I hear, from a throat that has had sandpaper taken to it, "It's OK. It's over. It's OK."

Against the alley wall, John rocks the boy in his arms. They both stare at me with a mix of fear, gratitude and horror. I'm not sure if John is talking to the boy or me. I try to stand and immediately collapse, pain shooting up my left leg. I roll onto my side, clutching my ankle and gritting my teeth.

"Easy now, Little Bird. You probably injured it when you jumped." He touches my arm tentatively.

"I forgot your dinner," I hiss out through clenched teeth. He is still for a moment, then throws his head back and roars laughter at the black sky. He gives my arm a hard squeeze.

"I reckon you're going to be OK."

"How about him?" We both look at the boy huddled against the wall. All big eyes and silence, he's starting to shake, shock setting in.

"I'll take care of him, you get yourself home." He returns to the boy, taking off his tattered coat and wrapping it around the child.

"The body," I say, gesturing at the mess without looking at it.

"We'll take care of it. You get yourself home and get some ice on that ankle."

"We?"

He winks at me, then cups his hands around his mouth and calls, "Yeep! Yeep! Whoop! Whoop! Yeep! Yeep! Whoop! Whoop!"

I stare at him. I'd almost forgotten he was a crazy homeless guy. Then I hear a distant echo. "Yeep. Yeep. Whoop. Whoop." It repeats two or three times from different directions. One was close.

"Get on home, Little Bird, death from above. Your part is done, for which I thank you. Is there someone you can call?"

Leaning against the side of the alley with one hand, I hobble almost back to the sidewalk, stopping just inside the alley. I slide down to sit on my bruised behind and dial one of the few numbers I know by heart. I get the feeling John and his associates do not want to be observed, so I keep my eyes down or pointed out into the street. After three rings he picks up.

"Preacher."

"I need a pickup," I say as flatly as I can. The pause is short.

"Just you?"

"Just me. You might want to put some plastic on your seats. I'm OK for now, but don't lallygag."

"Where are you?"

"In an alley off Ash. It's maybe the sixth alley from the Night Fowl. North."

"I'll be there in ten."

He will be. He is that kind of man. We've been through some shit together, Preacher and I. That's what I call him now, Preacher. It's a long ten minutes.

A Chevy Nova cruises to a stop on the curb opposite. The canary yellow paint job is perfect. Preacher swings open the big door, stands, spots me, and closes the door smoothly. He strides towards me without hesitation, a tall, pale man with dark wings of hair. He is wearing black jeans, a white button-down, a long black coat, and cracked black boots. In his left hand, he carries the sawed-off end of a pool cue, the thin end of which is sharpened to a point. I am now much less scared ... of vampires.

He stops two feet short of me and squats. His face is in darkness, so I can only imagine him examining me intently.

"The blood is not yours," he states.

I shake my head. "Unknown origin, recycled through a vamp. My ankle doesn't work, though. Sprained, not broken."

He nods sharply, then scoops me up in his arms and turns towards his car before I can protest. I decide not to and settle against his chest. He opens the back door and helps me slide in onto the crackling plastic.

"Elevate it," he says sharply, once I am in, and shuts the door. Gingerly I raise my leg and rest it on the door.

He starts the big engine, sending power thrumming through the steel frame of the car, and pulls smoothly away from the curb.

"You didn't tell me you were hunting tonight." There might or might not have been reproach in his voice. I don't say anything.

"How did it go wrong?"

"It was impromptu. Spotted a vampire taking food down an alley."

He stomps on the brakes, throwing me forward and sending pain spiking up my leg.

"Ow! Hey!"

He turns full around on the big bench seat and hangs over it to get his face in mine.

"Dammit, Penny, you stick to your method. You've got your weapon and your methodology. You stick to it, you survive, maybe. You improvise and you die. You know that." His nostrils are flaring and he is breathing a little fast.

"It was a kid," I say quietly.

"What?"

"It was a kid," I yell into his face, pushing mine even closer to his. "It was a little boy, you overbearing creep!"

"Penny..."

"But I should leave the rescuing to big, strong men like you, right? Only you weren't there, I was, and I couldn't let him eat that little boy." I'm shaking a little, fighting back tears. I am not going to cry, dammit. I fall back onto the plastic-covered seat, and fling my arm over my eyes. He is quiet for a moment.

"Where's the boy?" he asks softly.

"He's OK. He's with friends."

A couple of heartbeats later I hear him slide back down behind the steering wheel, and he puts the car back in drive. There's no more conversation on the drive to my apartment. He patiently helps me up the steps to my door, then turns to go. I hold onto the door frame with one hand and grab his shoulder with the other.

"Hey. Thanks." He looks back at me with eyes that aren't green or blue, but something in between.

"Take care, Penny. God Bless." And he's gone.

"You could have waited until I was safely in the door," I grumble to myself, fumbling with my keys and balancing on one foot. Finally, I push the door open and hop across the threshold. Oww! The bad ankle does not like jarring. I'm going to need crutches. I close the door and flip on the light. Pop. The light bulb blows. My shoulders sag. There is light from the street, and I can turn on the bathroom light and leave the door open. It's OK, Penny.

I really need to ice and elevate my ankle, but I have got to get these clothes off and rinse off the gore. I think once more about ways Preacher could have helped. My clothes are ruined. I strip them off and drop them on the bathroom floor. I hadn't realized how bad I smelled. Hot water pounds my skin, sluicing away blood, bits of flesh, and the sour smell of sweat and fear. God, I am surprised Preacher let me in his car, let alone picked me up. I wince when I think of his white shirt. No, I am not surprised. He is that kind of man.

When I finally begin to feel clean, I examine the port in my chest. I do not see any signs of damage. To be safe, I should probably ask the Good Doctor to clean the line. Crap. She won't be doing that for me now if our arrangement is really over.

Today is a miracle.

***

Dusk steals over the city, sending the good people of the world scurrying home, for dinner with the family and a walk with the dog. I drift comfortably towards wakefulness until I make the mistake of rolling over. Pain crashes over me in waves, making me catch my breath. It all comes back as a vivid half-dream, the alley, the boy, jumping out the window, stabbing and stabbing until my arms failed. Wake up, Penny, wake up and make it stop.

Sitting up is a struggle, accompanied by much cursing. I hurt everywhere, almost as if jumping out of a two-story window and landing on a vampire was a bad idea. How bad is it Penny, what have you done to yourself? My head feels like it is being split in two, my arms ache, my ribs complain with each breath, and I think I cracked a tooth, but everything seems to work, except my right ankle. Looking down at it where my feet rest on the floor, it's about three times the size of my left ankle. A dull roar of pain travels up my leg when I try to move my foot the least little bit, and I almost black out. I take the deepest breaths I can, the pain in my ribs distracting some from my ankle. Is it broken? How would I tell?

I let my eyes wander away from my injury, and just inside the door, on the floor, is a piece of notebook paper. From here I can see it has writing on it, but I can not read it. Gingerly I ease myself down onto my hands and knees and begin the slow crawl to find out what it is. Penny, you are such an idiot. This is why there are no real heroes, it hurts too much. Finally, I am above the piece of paper and can read it, still on all fours. The handwriting is Preacher's.

Provisions outside the door. Busy next couple days. Call if emergency.

Opening the door is one more struggle. A pair of crutches that must have been leaning against the door slide down and almost hit me on the head, clattering on the hardwood floor. Just outside is a cardboard box, which I slide inside as quickly as I can, not wanting to be seen this way by someone in the hall. Once I have the door shut and locked, I open it and look inside. On top is a bottle of hydrocodone, an elastic bandage and a reusable cold pack. Under that appears to be all food: cans of soup, a small loaf of dark bread, crackers, peanut butter, and three oranges. There is even a can opener. Oh, and a box of tea. Lucky for me, taking care of people is what Preacher does. There's a cost, of course. I feel my freedom slipping away from me again.

Suddenly I realize how hungry I am. Every movement hurts, as I get the box slid over next to the stove, get a pot from under the sink, open a can and pour the soup in. I expend a little more energy to put the kettle on. Doing all this while trying to use the crutches is some kind of grim comedy routine. Too bad there's no one to appreciate it. After eating the soup, some crackers and an orange, I settle gingerly back onto the bed with my tea.

My journal is on the bedside table. It is bound in green cloth, and it is old. I hold it to my face and inhale the smell. The first pages contain someone else's memories, but I leave them, and append mine afterwards. I flip past the pages that already have writing on them until

I get to the entries for the last vamp, turning pages more slowly now, skimming entries about spotting him the first time, observing his kills, learning his preferences, his favorite hunting grounds. I read slower when I get to the account of finally taking him, of baiting the trap with myself, myself also being the trap. When he plunges his fangs into me, my First Bite wakes up and begins to burn, and there is a faint echo in my neck. It is a more familiar and a sweeter pain, distracting me from these injuries at least a little. When I get to the end of the account, I pick up a pen and start to date the next entry, but I realize I have no idea what day it is. I am not sure I want to relive that, anyway. There is little else to do but hobble over to the box, get a couple of hydrocodone, and wash them down with the last swallow of my tea. I drift into a warm, fuzzy oblivion.

7

GEEZER

Bill is up early, or what passes for early these days. They all seem to sleep more the longer they are in this place. The staff still lets him shower himself, small mercies, and he had shaved. Slapping on the aftershave, that smell dissolves forty years, and he is back in the department store with his Betty slapping his face with it for the first time. She does it harder than necessary, then laughs at him when he flinches and grabs her arm. She was not always the kindest person, but he could not resist that sly little smile she got when she was about to be bad, and she sure could be good to him when she chose. You old fool. It is hard enough to tie a tie with arthritic fingers, let alone all misty-eyed.

It's Sunday morning, so the dining room is lively. If you are one of the lucky ones, this is the day for visitors. Some residents even go to church with their families, and everyone comes back after for brunch. Children are underfoot, threatening to trip geezers who wouldn't survive a broken hip. His Charlie only comes at Christmas. He had tried, but he had botched being a father. Especially after she passed. He had too much of his own grief to take on a little boy's. Damn, why is he so maudlin today?

Frank and Gilbert are already at their table, the one closest to the door. Frank has his coffee, black with one sugar, and Gilbert his juice and bran muffin, which he eats by tearing off little chunks with his thumb and forefinger. They both drive Bill nuts. Outside, he doubted they would have been friends. In here they are literally life savers. Bickering with them over cards, complaining about the food together, lamenting that they had not died young, these things give him a reason to get out of bed.

This morning, there is another reason. When they see him, they start the slow process of getting up from the table. Gilbert bangs his walker noisily against his chair but does not grimace like he does on other days. Together they shuffle out the door and down the sidewalk to the bench under the sign that reads, Golden Years Assisted Living. They take their seat with various amounts of creaking and groaning. It is pleasant to sit in the sun.

After an hour of waiting, Bill desperately needs to pee, and the cheerfulness is fading.

"I don't think she's coming," Frank finally says.

"She's only missed two Sundays in the past year," Gilbert says and looks at Bill.

Bill shrugs. "Shit happens. Could be she can't make it."

"Oh my goodness," from Frank. He's looking at the corner where she always comes into view. There she is, in the same tight mini-skirt and white little top as always. Today she is on crutches, though, one foot held gingerly off the ground. They openly stare as she limps past, she pretends not to notice. Frank mutters, "I wonder what happened?"

"That's a shame, a cryin' shame," Gilbert replies.

When she is about ten feet past them, she stops and drops her little purse. Together they stare as she slowly bends from the waist, ass in the air, and leisurely picks it up. She teeters a bit, one foot off the ground, leaning on one crutch, and they hold their breath. Then she straightens up and begins hobbling along again. Gilbert breathes out his standard prayer, "Bless her, that's why I'm still alive."

***

Bill leans on the parapet wall of the roof, Gilbert beside him, the concrete rough against his paper-thin old man skin. Sometimes after their angel has passed, they make their way up here and try to catch one more glimpse of her right before she enters the park. Today it was taking her longer than usual, no doubt because of the crutches.

"What do you think happened to her?" asks Gilbert.

Bill spits over the side, watching it float down several stories before losing it. "Life is dangerous."

Gilbert nods. "She doesn't give the impression of someone overly cautious." He pauses. "Did you hear Harold fell in the shower and busted his leg?"

"Jeanne told me," Bill answers.

"What are the odds that a truck is coming for him tonight?" Gilbert asks.

"High."

"Do we Kevorkian him before they drag him off to do god knows what to him?"

Bill sighs. "He's a skeptic. He won't take it."

"The tracker, then. I'll try to plant it on him at dinner."

Bill nods. After a minute, he says, "I'm considering a little obstructionism."

Gilbert looks at him. "Fuck with the truck? Won't save Harold, long term."

"No, but it will make me feel just a little bit better."

Gilbert chuckles. "I'm in."

They see her then, her white top blazing in the sun. After she disappears under the trees, Gilbert slaps Bill on the back and starts shuffling towards the stairs. Bill stays. The roof is one of his favorite places. The usable space is divided in half by an island of mechanical equipment, the elevator, HVAC and other building systems. The other side of the roof is set up nicer because it is more sheltered from the weather. This side has two pigeon-shit-encrusted lounge chairs protected by a rickety umbrella. He has brought a beach towel to partially cover the bird shit and a can of Coke. He settles onto one of the chairs and closes his eyes. For a while, memories form an impressionistic movie in his mind. First is the recent memory of the young woman on crutches, sweaty and struggling down the street, so much of her beautiful legs visible. When she leaned over on the crutches to pick up her purse, she was like a bird with a broken wing reaching for a worm. A bird with the best ass he has ever seen. He hopes her ankle is not hurting too much.

The movie shifts to the first time he saw his wife, a rainy day in the city, and her struggling to get her groceries onto the bus. He had helped her, not because he was gallant, but because her clothes clung to her in a way that made him want to be close to her. That wicked smile she had given him that told him she knew exactly why he was helping her, and that she was fine with it. The images flow by his mind's eye, her white hot fury when his mother said she couldn't come to the house dressed like that, then her kindness towards his mother when his mother took ill, not knowing her own illness was not far off. Her puking on his shoes and cursing that she had never wanted a child and it was his fault. The beatific smile, happiest he had ever seen her, when she held Peter for the first time. Her despair when he shipped out, and her relief when he returned to find her health already fading. His eyes might have been damp when he drifted off.

Raised voices wake him. First, he is murkily aware of them penetrating his oblivion. Then there are recognizable fragments of speech: "...thought we agreed ... six months changes things ...ruin something that's working..." He opens his eyes a crack. A young man and woman, both in the uniform of the establishment, are standing close together, spitting words at each other, apparently trying to redefine their relationship. He chuckles, maybe louder than he should have.

"What's that? You got something to say, old man?"

He laughs harder. Soon the red-faced young man is standing over him, fists clenched at his sides.

"What are you laughing at, old man?"

"Me when I was you, Son. Me when I was you."

Bill rolls onto his side with a groan.

"Don't mind me. You'll figure it out, or you won't. Makes no difference to me."

"Come on, Baby, forget about him. He's just a pathetic old dude. Leave him alone, let's go find some real privacy."

When they had been gone long enough he was pretty sure he wouldn't meet them on the stairs, he sat up stiffly. It was always stiffly, anymore. He should head down and wash up for supper. He had slept clear through afternoon snack and he would need his strength later.

***

It is dark in the alley. There should be a light above the loading dock, but someone keeps stealing the bulb. Bill leans against the still warm brick, waiting in the darkness. He can't see Gilbert across the alley and screened by a dumpster. Bill has a rolling oxygen tank with him, the mask dangling around his neck. That had been a last-minute idea of Gilbert's, and luckily the supply closet had a shitty lock. Not luck, really. Everything about the home was low-grade crap, if you looked past the new paint and shiny linoleum.

In the distance, Bill thinks he hears a sharp, "yawp yawp." Yes, there it is again, a little closer. He straightens up and looks over at the dumpster. Gilbert gives him two staccato flashes from the flashlight also lifted from the supply closet. The next, "yawp yawp", comes from the entrance to the alley. Bill pulls the oxygen mask over his mouth and nose, grabs the handle of the rolling tank, and begins to shuffle in front of the loading dock just as headlights turn down the alley.

He is directly in front of the dock and unzipping his pants with an only partly faked palsy, when the big truck brakes squeal through the drone of a diesel engine. Blinded by the headlights, he hears a truck door open and cursing from that direction. He has his member out and is willing it to do its job, but that is iffy these days.

"Come on," he mutters.

Then a hand grabs him by the shoulder and yanks him around. Apparently, that jolt was what the system needed, and a warm stream of piss sprays out all over the man's boots.

"Christ!" The man jumps back.

"What's going on?" asks a voice from the truck.

"Old fucker peed all over me."

"What, on purpose? He trying to interfere?"

Bill still can't see because of the headlights in his face. He should have thought of that when making the plan. He doesn't know if Gilbert is done driving a nail into the back tire of the truck, so he stares as blankly as he can into the lights, hoping for a sign.

"Nah, he's like my Uncle Pete. He probably doesn't even know where he is."

"Maybe we should take him too," jeers the voice from the truck.

"You know we can only pick up what's on the manifest," the one right in front of Bill replies. "OK, Gramps, put that back in your pants and let's get you out of the way." The man takes hold of the oxygen tank handle and gives Bill a gentle push. Bill takes one step away from the loading dock. He has to keep distracting them if Gilbert is in the open, but he still can't see.

"Whooooo ....Whoooooo" drifts down from one of the rooftops.

"What, we got fuckin' owls in the city now?" says the man in the truck.

Bill breathes a sigh of relief and gets his dick back in his pants.

"Must eat the pigeons, like the hawks," answers the man with his hand on Bill's shoulder.

Bill puts his hand on the oxygen tank handle and begins to shuffle in the direction the man wants him to go, but after only a few steps, he trips over the cord running from the tank to the mask on his face. Pain blooms in his hands and knees as he catches himself on the rough alley paving. The oxygen tank slams down heavily next to him, and metallic pieces fly off. The hiss of escaping gas is loud.

"Shit! Shit! Shit!" from the man standing over him.

"You've done it now," shouts the man in the truck.

"That stuff is flammable as hell," a note of panic in his voice as he backs away.

"Let's get the fuck out of here," and the truck begins backing down the alley. Bill hears running feet, and soon both the man and the truck are gone. He remains on hands and knees, until the hissing of escaping gas stops. It takes a long time. When it finally stops, Gilbert gets a hand under one of his armpits and helps him to his feet. His pajamas are shredded and bloody at the knees, and he doesn't want to look at his hands.

"Whooee! You sure did give them a fright. I bet some Capo has to find himself some new drivers."

Bill grunts. "I doubt they get out that easy." He grins then. "Fubared their schedule for tonight, though."

Before they leave the alley, Bill turns back to the dark canyon between buildings and calls, "Ollie Ollie Oxen Free."

8

— ◆ —

BAD PENNY

I wake a few minutes before the alarm. Bright, cheerful sunshine blares obnoxiously into my eyes. I groan, but Sunday is my community service day, and that gets me out of bed. Today is the day I make the world a little better, a little easier to bear. Knowing this puts a bounce in my step, even on crutches, though the crutches are going to make it interesting.

From my Sunday drawer, I select a black vinyl miniskirt and a white Lycra top, both skin tight. No bra. Black canvas sneakers, because they will fit over the bandage on my ankle. A crutch under each shoulder, and I'm ready to do good. I snap open the deadbolt on the door and sally forth.

Almost colliding with a shambling figure in the hall. A young man, he mumbles something that might be, "Excuse me." Then as he stumbles down the hall, he begins yelling and casting dark looks back over his shoulder at me. His speech is slurred, unintelligible. I give him time to get far ahead of me. Some kid still drunk from Saturday night.

When I get to the stairs, he's standing three or four steps down, leaning against the wall. I hesitate. He makes eye contact and starts speaking. He's hard to understand. I catch something about how he shouldn't take it out on me, and something like, "... my cousin beat me down and back ..." He hadn't been stumbling, he was limping. When he talks, it looks like there is blood on his teeth, and his mouth appears swollen.

Slowly I ease past him, taking the steps with care. He reaches out a hand and rests it lightly on my shoulder. I do not react. I think he's trying to help stabilize me. He accompanies me all the way down the stairs. He keeps apologizing, I keep forgiving him. When we get to the small, dreary lobby, he sits on the floor in a corner, curling up into a ball. I don't ask him if he wants me to call the police, or a cab to take him to the hospital. I swing out into a bright Sunday morning.

I stop outside the doors and spit, trying to get this bitter taste out of my mouth. This is my cheerful fucking morning. I'm still getting used to the crutches. Luckily, it's not far to the Sunday spot. At the first intersection, I round the corner and there they are, sitting on the bench in front of the building with the Golden Years Assisted Living sign. Three old men lined up on that bench like birds on a wire. They quickly turn their heads and pretend they aren't watching for me. It's harder than usual for them because it takes me so long. As I pass I hear muttering, "...what happened...think...hurt...shame..." When I've made it about ten feet past them, I stop and drop my silly little purse on the sidewalk. Relishing the expectant hush, I slip the crutches out from under my arms, and I slowly bend from the waist, knees straight, ass in the air, to pick up my bag. I have to use my other hand to balance with that crutch. I slowly straighten up, and I hear the ritual incantation, repeated each week. "I'm tellin' ya man, that's why I'm still alive."

I hobble down the street, a silly grin on my face.

It's a bright, beautiful morning. Normally I'd be chilly, especially in this outfit, but hobbling along on crutches is work. I'm sweaty, tired and sore when I reach the park where Preacher does his thing. Something is different today. There is the usual congregation of homeless, junkies and prostitutes, plus a few fascinated dog walkers, ogling from a distance. What stands out is the busy little knot of activity next to the bench Preacher speaks from. About a dozen citizens with the shine still on have installed a portable stage. Next to it are three folding tables, with two busy bodies sitting behind each on folding chairs. They have stacks of paper in front of them. I do not see Preacher at first, but then I see the back of his head. He's standing at the front of his ragtag congregation, watching.

Their champion, apparently here to contest with Preacher for some grubby souls, steps onto the stage like he owns it. He is wearing blue jeans and a blue button-down with the cuffs rolled up. Striding up to the microphone, this pretender beams at us.

"Good morning, Folks. It's such a pleasure to be here with you this beautiful morning, in one of our city's public spaces." He spreads his arms to take in the park. He has a fine, warm voice and a genuine smile. Mentally I hang a sign around his neck that says, "Dead Meat."

"We are here today to talk about second chances." He gestures to a banner behind him that reads, Department of Second Chances. "As you know, Mayor Broadridge's compassionate leadership has harnessed this city's can-do spirit to lift up all our citizens. We all deserve a fair shot, and let's be honest, most of us need a second chance sometime in our lives, whether we think we deserve it or not. I am here to tell you, you deserve it."

He pauses at this point for breath, and to let us have a chance to applaud while he beams at us. Hostile silence is what he gets. He nods his head to show that he understands.

"Throughout history, charlatans and false saviors have preyed on the down-and-out. Many of them claim to be men of God."

He looks right at Preacher. He's got balls.

"What do they offer you? Guilt? Salt for your wounds? They answer your thirst with fire and brimstone. They do not care for you, they prey on your insecurities. They do not want you to improve your lot, they profit by your sorrow."

There are boos and hisses from the crowd, but I also hear a few, "Let him talk."

"The Department of Second Chances is your fellow man reaching out to help you through the tool of government. A combination of long term shelters, health care, professional counseling and job training helps people like yourselves overcome the root causes of their poverty, and develop the tools to be productive members of society."

The pretender pauses to beam at us and let us bask in his personal warmth. The man is like a sun, lighting the space around him and pulling people into his orbit.

Preacher leaps onto his bench. He turns to face his congregation, black coat swirling about him. His shirt is blindingly white. Raising both hands above his head, he speaks in a rhythmic cadence.

"The Psalmist says, 'Thy rod and thy staff, they comfort me.'"

The pretender smirks.

"Tools of punishment and control. That's what he offers you. An abusive father, is that what you need? How about being lifted up on the strong shoulders of your brothers and sisters." Honey on his tongue.

Preacher's voice rings out.

"He maketh me to lie down in green pastures: he leadeth me beside the still waters."

"Every one of you started out with a dream," croons the Pretender. "But you have lost it, haven't you? We at the City offer you concrete assistance to getting that dream back."

"Our Father which art in Heaven, Hallowed be thy name, Thy Kingdom come, Thy will be done in Earth, as it is in Heaven."

It's hard to look away from Preacher, standing like a pillar of iron, eyes burning. With an effort, I turn my head to look at the pretender, when I hear his smooth, warm voice.

"You can be a productive member of society again, and be respected for it. You can belong. All it takes to get started is to fill out some forms here with my colleagues from the Department of Second Chances." He points to the eager, fresh-faced individuals behind the folding tables, stacks of paper in front of them.

"He asks you to trade your Faith for paperwork. When did filling out a form ever set your feet on the straight and narrow?"

The bureaucrats behind the tables exchange sullen glances. Preacher's congregation is uneasy, winos shifting their weight from foot to foot, working girls eyeing the newcomers for potential clients. The Pretender maintains his smile, but I see a crease between his brows. He speaks, that pleasing timbre rolling over the crowd.

"With education, re-socialization, and professional counseling, you can leave the grim streets behind, get a job, find a clean, safe place to live and feed your family. Join us in the land of plenty that is your birthright." He holds his hand out to the crowd in invitation.

Preacher continues to disdain looking at the interlopers. His eyes probe his congregation, leaving nowhere to hide for people whom he has pulled from the gutter and wiped the vomit off of. Women he has defended from scumbag boyfriends or pimps. Men he has knocked down to prevent them from hurting their children and regretting it forever.

"You and I know, brothers and sisters, how easy life is. When has filling out a form ever fixed anything real?"

"There are those who think you are broken." The pretender points at Preacher next to him on his bench. "They think you are flawed, and that is why you suffer. We in the administration reject their judgmental dismissal of those less fortunate. You have been stepped on and pushed aside. What you need, what you deserve, is a helping hand and someone to do what no one else ever did for you, teach you how to be successful. How to find a job. How to keep a job. How to get an education. And yes, how to navigate the labyrinth of paperwork and bureaucracy that are an unavoidable part of modern life."

Almost before he stops speaking, Preacher's voice rings out.

"Will a job training program stay your hand when your heart hungers for evil?"

There are a few mumbled no's from the crowd.

"Will knowing how to walk and talk in polite society bolster up your will when your vices are pounding on your brain like hammers?"

The "no's" are louder this time. The pretender tries to counter, sounding calm and reasonable.

"This is melodrama."

Preacher stretches his arms out to his sides, palms facing the crowd. His voice is the hammer striking the anvil.

"When your own inner beast rouses itself, flooding your heart with darkness, will you turn to a counselor for a pep talk, or a preacher who will put iron in your soul?"

"Preacher," the congregation roars. I realize I am leaning precariously forward when I stumble. Preacher drops his arms to his sides and steps off his bench. His congregation swarms forward to hug him, slap him on the back, and shake his hand.

I look at the pretender. He has a small, tight smile on his face. He turns to his crowd, who are puzzled and stunned. He shrugs.

"Let's pack it up. We'll be meeting at the Grounded in an hour, for a discussion. Monica, the owner, told me Mocha's are the Sunday Special. Our topic this week is seeking justice in an unjust world. Hope to see you all there." He begins dismantling the sound system.

It's going to be a while before I can get to Preacher, so I watch the pretender. He moves with precision and economy of effort. Competence and confidence roll out from him in gentle waves. My hostility at his trying to break Preacher's balls is fading, now that Preacher has triumphed. When he steps down off his stage and heads for the thinning knot of people around Preacher, I hobble towards them.

Preacher's congregation has begun to dissipate. Many of them will be headed for the soup kitchen. A few will volunteer to help Preacher the rest of the morning and afternoon. When dark falls, they will return to haunting their haunts. A few of them notice the pretender's approach and move to stand at Preacher's back.

The pretender strides right up to Preacher and sticks out his hand.

"I guess you know your crowd, Preacher."

Preacher ignores the proffered hand.

"They are not my crowd, they are my flock."

The pretender smiles tolerantly, oblivious to the threat written in every line of Preacher's body.

"Don't get me wrong, we are both genuine in our beliefs, I'm sure, but preaching is a performance. You know it for certain, you were fantastic."

Sensing the rage building behind Preacher's eyes, I hobble forward to try and prevent bloodshed. The pretender sees me approach. He tilts his head, observing a phenomenon, that bemused smile still on his face.

"And here's one of your black sheep."

I give him my most wicked smile. "All loaded up with sin and in need of correction."

Preacher looks at me for the first time.

"Miss Penny might dress like a slut, but she does the Lord's work, intentionally or not."

Now its my turn to be angry. I step up to Preacher and press my body full against him, staring up into his eyes.

"That's right. I'm not good, but I'm good for something."

Preacher's face drains of blood, and he takes a stumbling step back, knocking over one of his honor guard. If I didn't know better, I'd say he was on the verge of trembling. The pretender looks at him quizzically.

"Preacher?" with a note of concern in his voice.

Preacher locks those two pieces of burning sea he calls eyes with mine.

"Miss Penny knew me ... during dark times. She reminds me that I owe her ..."

"Courtesy," I finish for him. I'm glad I have these crutches to hold onto or I would be shaking. I turn a shaky smile to the pretender.

"The bad old days are long gone." He's back to bemused.

"I'm sure. We've all been there, right?" He sneaks a look at Preacher out of the corner of his eye, then back to me.

"Do you need a ride somewhere? You'd be welcome to come to Discussion Hour. Mocha on me. Then I can give you a lift anywhere. Looks like you're having some trouble getting around." He nods at the crutches. Is he oblivious to his peril? I intentionally do not look at Preacher. The pretender winks at me. The idiot is baiting him on purpose. I turn what feels like a sickly smile on Preacher.

"I wouldn't be getting around at all if it weren't for Preacher."

He nods. "You'll come to the soup kitchen."

"I haven't heard the lady make her choice," says the pretender, turning towards Preacher, not aggressive, but not meek.

Preacher raises an eyebrow. The casual observer might think that he'd calmed down.

"Now she's a Lady?"

"You two work out who has the biggest dick. I'm going home."

I turn my back on both of them and hobble towards the edge of the park. Leaving a tense silence in my wake, I put my lips together and whistle. It's a little tune of my own, alternately cheerful and mournful. No one follows me.

Halfway home, pride feels like folly. My arms shake each time I put weight on them to take a step. My armpits are starting to chafe, and my good leg is cramping. It is that midway point in a journey where you wish you'd never started, but it's too late to do anything but tough it out to the finish.

Here comes a bus stop. The thought of being crammed in with all that other meat makes me nauseous. I just don't think I can make it on foot. Luckily as a waitress, I always have dollar bills. I limp up to the stop.

I stop at an unfriendly distance, but that does not save me from scrutiny. My sweat-soaked shirt is now practically see-through, and I'm flushed and breathing hard. Not to mention the amount of thigh I'm showing. And there's the limp, and the pheromones I'm sweating out. I feel the collective hunger of my prospective travelers beginning to reach for me. Frankly, I'm a danger to others and myself.

A muscular yellow car slides to the curb in front of the bus stop, and purrs throatily. A middle-aged man in a well-tailored suit and CEO hair raps on the driver's side window.

"You can't park in front of the bust stop, punk."

The big door opens, pushing the Citizen away from the car. Preacher steps out and ignores him. His eyes meet mine, then travel down every inch of me, and back to my eyes.

There is a squeal of brakes, and a horn blows directly in my ear. The bus stops inches from Preacher's bumper. Getting in that car is not necessarily safer, but the devil you know..." I hop to the passenger side and get in, taking three tries to get the crutches into the back seat. Preacher's presence buffers me from the blaring horns and shouted abuse. I shut the door with a grunt and lean back into the seat. I feel the car pull into traffic.

I'm tense and wary for the first minute or so. Head back, eyes closed, I count breaths. Like the crowd at the bus stop, I can sense forces swirling inside him. I can also feel his iron control. It's OK. The tension drains away, letting the fatigue and pain back in.

"You need to lie low for a while," Preacher says, looking straight ahead.

"Look, I know you are pissed I broke protocol and jumped that vamp, but I told you why. Drop it."

"He has been missed, Penny. He was somebody."

"What, you mean nobody ever missed the other vampires I offed?"

"Vampires disappear. It is expected. But some individuals are more notable than others."

"So he was hot shit, huh? Some kind of royalty?"

"More of an ambassador."

"What, he was chief vampire envoy to the United Nations of Nasties?" I get a scowl for that one.

"There is one member of the Family that serves as an adviser and emissary to the Vampire Mayor."

My mouth drops open.

"Vampire mobsters?"

"A younger son of the Boss, turned in his early 20's."

"What the Hell?"

"It is not wise to send a vampire to live among humans, so the Mayor sends one of his bound humans. It is an exchange to cement cooperation and peace between rival predators." He pauses while turning. "You need to look beyond yourself sometimes, Penny."

"Christ on a stick, I've had enough of your superiority today."

"Blaspheming achieves nothing."

"It pisses you off." Frowning, I consider the implications.

"So the Vampire Mayor has to tell the big boss mobster that his son is missing."

The car purrs to a stop at the curb in front of my apartment building. I put my hand on top of his.

"Thanks for warning me."

With a sharp nod, he pulls his hand away and puts it on the steering wheel, looking straight ahead out the windshield. I look through the window, and seeing the entrance to my building, ask him a question.

"Can I have one of your cards? There's someone in my building" ... I shrug ... "might need some help."

He reaches into the inside pocket of his coat, giving me a knife-edge smile. "I thought you didn't trust in Him."

"I trust in you."

He hands me a business card, heavy white stock, with only this printed on it. "I can help." And a phone number. Not the one I call.

"Thanks." I drop it in my purse, open my door and swing my legs out.

"Penny."

I look back over my shoulder.

"Thanks for coming."

I grin. "Wouldn't miss the show."

I get out and close my door. Preacher gets out of his side and retrieves my crutches from his back seat. He hands them to me, and without another word, gets in the car and drives.

I struggle up the stairs, check the trip alarm on the door, and stumble into my abode. I want to collapse on my bed, but I know I need to eat something. I cut an orange into wedges and eat those before I strip off my clothes, limp to my bed and plunge into oblivion.

9

— • —

VAMPIRE MAYOR

The Vampire Mayor is humming and rocking slowly from foot to foot. This is his happy place, away from the noise and chaos of the office. The warehouse is dark except for the giant mobile that spins slowly overhead. It is his own design. Plexiglas coffins, filled with embalming fluid and softly silhouetted corpses, rise and fall silently as they circle. Each one holds one of his favorite kills, outlined in soft light, like a halo. These are his memories.

A metal door slides noisily open, letting in the sounds of traffic and the smells of the evening, car exhaust and cooking smells mingling. A young man in a suit drags an old man in by his arm. The old man stumbles and shuffles, and is dressed in institutional pajamas.

Got your meal, Mr. Mayor, Sir."

"Mayor or Sir," the Mayor replies.

"What?"

"Either Mr. Mayor or Sir, not both."

"Uh, OK, Mr. Mayor." He shuffles his feet. "Sir."

The old man cackles. "Jesus, what a dumb lump. If I were fifteen years younger he'd a been toast soon as he tried to grab me. Would've snapped his arm like a twig."

The vampire smiles, and the old man flinches. "I have no doubt. That is why you are going to be such a treat. Like they were," the vampire says. He points upward. The old man looks up. His eyes go wide and he trembles, but his voice is steady when he responds.

"You think I didn't see worse living on the streets? One kind of butcher is like another."

"Oh, but there you are wrong," the Vampire Mayor says, looking up and lifting his hands in benediction. "Each of these was more than a kill, more than a meal. Most vampires favor young prey because the raw vitality is fire in their freezing veins. But I have learned to appreciate the old." His gaze lowers to the old man. "You contain a lifetime of experience, love, loss, joy, grief. I will cradle you as a lover while I slowly sip away everything unique about you."

The old man honks a loogie. "Then I suppose you'll fuck yourself with my giant penis and cry because you got a pencil dick."

The vampire throws his head back and laughs, which always has an effect on people. The old man drops to his knees, hands covering his ears. Gently the Mayor picks him up, a bundle of brittle bones and memories. He squirms like an infant or a small pet. Before biting, the Vamp presses his face against the old man's throat and inhales, filling his nose with the slightly sweet, musty smell of old man. Saliva fills his mouth, and he tenderly eases his fangs under the skin and into the generous artery. His mouth is filled with the most rancid taste he has ever encountered. He yanks his fangs out, spitting. It is the Old Man's turn to laugh.

"Been eating kimchi all week. It's the only thing I can taste anymore."

He laughs and laughs, until he stops.

10

BAD PENNY

Monday sundown, time to rise. I cut an orange into wedges. I used to be an apple person because it was too much work to peel oranges. Then I hit on the method of cutting the orange into narrow wedges, and I am now a citrus freak. Good thing, too. Helps me absorb iron, and I'm always borderline anemic. I chase the orange with a fistful of vitamins, then limp over to one of the bookcases that line the walls. If I plan to be reclining with my foot up all night, I need something to occupy me.

A tentative knock brings me back with a snap. Breathing a little fast, I pick up one crutch and limp to my bed, pull my sharpened pool cue out from under it, and limp to the door. Almost no one knows where I live. Preacher, of course, but he does not do anything tentatively. Even my employer doesn't know where I live. I look through the peephole, then sigh and open the door. Before I can say anything, Francis blurts it out.

"I know you told me never to come here, but I was worried."

He looks like hell. Disheveled, unshaven, with dark circles under his eyes, and even a little dried food on his collar. An unhappy Francis pays my bills, but if he crashes and burns he is no good to me. Plus he is carrying two coffees from Joe's, and a brown paper bag. I turn sideways and nod him in.

"Enter my lair at your own risk."

His sickly, uncertain smile makes an appearance. Stepping a few paces past me, he turns and frowns at the bandage on my ankle.

"You're hurt."

"Ten points towards your Sherlock badge," said with a smile. He does a cute little head duck. I like myself for stringing him along to support my habit, like myself a lot. "Have a seat," I say, limping toward my old Formica-topped table. He puts the coffees and bag on the table and pulls out a chair. I sit across from him and raise an eyebrow.

"One of those coffees for me?"

"Yes." He shoves the cardboard tray towards me. "I know it's late for coffee, but I figured you're kind of a night owl and this might be like your morning." He crosses his arms on the table in front of him, then leans back in the chair, instead. I take a coffee and push the tray and second coffee back towards him.

"What's in the bag?"

"Oh, uh, that was Tom's idea."

"Tom's?"

"I was talking to him about maybe coming to see if you were OK. I said I might bring you some coffee."

While he is talking, I pull a bottle of amber liquid out of the paper bag.

"I'm not a bourbon drinker. I hope it's OK," he says.

I unscrew the cap and swig from the bottle. It is cheap, harsh, and warm as it slides down my throat and pools in my stomach.

"Tastes like it's from the right bottle to me." I hold it out towards him. He shakes his head. Taking the lid off my coffee, I pour too much in. His small, nervous hands are on the table in front of him now.

"You look like someone ran over your puppy. Fighting with the missus again?"

He blows a puff of air out of his nose.

"Right. She'd have to stop pretending I was dead."

"Ouch. Silent treatment?"

"Sometimes I have to leave the house and bump into someone on the sidewalk just to prove I'm not a ghost. My only way to be part of my daughter's life is to listen from another room when she plays piano. And Becky, she scoots so far away from me on the bed, I keep waiting for her to fall off the edge."

I take the lid off his coffee and pour in bourbon. He leans on the table with both elbows.

"The thing is, Penny, if I had done something bad, if I'd hit her or blown all our money gambling or ..." He was going to say, "cheated on her," but he looks down at his coffee for a moment, then back up. "Then at least I'd understand. Maybe I could even make it up to them. But this, this is killing me a little every day."

Screw the coffee. I swig from the bottle again.

"Maybe you should leave." He gets even more pale. "She has a good job, right? It's not like they'd be out on the street without you."

"I don't...Jesus, Penny, I ... who would I be?" He looks utterly lost. "No, I...I can't."

I shrug. "It's your hell. Better drink up."

We get a nice buzz. I tell him a few dirty jokes, lean on the table to give him a look down my shirt, try to get that despair off his face. Then I pack him off. At the door, I touch his elbow.

"It's sweet that you were worried, Francis, and I do have one problem. "

"What? Is it something I can help with?"

"With the work I've missed, I'm not going to have my rent. I'm short 200."

He smiles. "I thought it might be something like that." He fumbles with his wallet. "I came prepared, see." He carefully counts a stack of bills into his hand, then looks up eagerly. "Here's 200, and another 20 for, you know, whatever."

I take the bills. "Thanks. Now you best be off."

"Right. Good night, Penny." His last grin is a sly one I have not seen before. "I guess if I'm helping pay the rent, I can stop by now and then." He leaves me standing in my doorway with a smile on my face so brittle it must be porcelain.

***

This one has a website, deliciousregret.com, that sells Goth clothing, designer kink. She's her own model, and an exquisite corpse she is, showed to great advantage in lush black and white photography. Clever. It picks up all the details of her perfect form, without giving away her unnatural complexion.

I was trolling, looking for new prey, the first time I saw her. The Dome Room was as good as any place. Dark and crowded means good cover, and is something like an all-you-can-eat buffet. They usually do not gorge, however. One-on-one they are formidable, but they are quickly destroyed if discovered by too many humans. Care must be taken.

She was something of a minor celebrity. The limelight is a strange place for a vampire, even the dim light of local fame. There is a stage in the Dome Room, raised in the middle of the floor. Perhaps intended for live bands once, it's been claimed by the dancers, regulars usually, exhibitionists who can dance and know it. That night, instead of the usual gaggle of show-offs on stage, Dark Violet had it to herself.

Vampires have an odd grace, not completely mammalian. Usually, I think of it as human with a little reptilian mixed in. Sinuous, almost boneless, with joints that move in ways not explained by Gray's Anatomy. Dark Violet was like that, but with something else thrown in, perhaps Great Heron. Her Reptilian Bird Woman dance was mesmerizing. Every eye in the place was on her, including mine. I didn't need the familiar itch of my First Bite to know I was watching something not human. We all knew, but we didn't care.

The black braid of her long hair was like an extension of her whip-lean body. Her long legs were bare and rippled with wiry strength. Eyes closed, and she wore a rapturous and startlingly toothy smile on her angular face. I had never known a vampire to express pleasure when not hunting or feeding, but it was pure joy I was seeing on that stage. Taking her would be a new kind of thrill.

The music segued into another song and she stopped instantaneously, limbs akimbo. Then she was nothing but a blur as she leapt off the stage and knifed through the crowd. I made sure to keep the crowd between her and me. I was not ready for her to see me yet, not until I knew who she was. Not her name, but what she liked, how she hunted, what circles she traveled in, and where she nested. To my surprise, she headed directly for wannabe land. They were the ones who wanted to belong at the Dome Room, but didn't. They were attracted to the scene, inescapably drawn to it, even, but just couldn't be that person who put on those clothes and dove into the sweaty, undulating, claustrophobic crowd. They might own the clothes, ordered online, and have worn them in front of the mirror, but nowhere else. They lurked, almost creepily, at the cluster of tiny tables in a corner, drinking watered down, overpriced drinks, and radiating envy and longing.

They were almost as hungry as vampires. Perhaps that made them juicy.

I had expected Dark Violet to dive into the tightly packed throng. It was beautiful camouflage, and target rich. She had eyes only for the wannabes, however. They seemed to expect her, vacating chairs as she approached so that she might sit, rising to hug her with clinging embraces, holding on too long. Are they her Bound? Is she so bold as to bring them out with her as an entourage? Or are they simply the herd from which she feeds, gathered at this watering hole in their psychic desert?

Over the course of the next hour, four or five daring souls tried to approach her. She ignored them completely. One cock-of-the-walk refused to believe she could ignore him and reached for her shoulder. I expected to see his arm broken, but not the way it happened. A woman in a black skirt and white button-down rose swiftly from the chair next to Dark Violet, grabbed his arm in some kind of lock, and snapped his elbow. I could faintly hear his scream above the noise of the club. Platinum hair escaping from its neat bun, she forced him to his knees, still holding the broken arm. Dark Violet gave her would-be suitor a bemused look and waved a bouncer towards her table.

Once the bouncer had taken charge of the wounded miscreant, Dark Violet drew her defender into her lap. With one finger, she traced the line of the trembling woman's jaw, continuing down her throat and the line of buttons on her shirt. Tenderly she pushed the woman's askew glasses back onto the bridge of her nose. I would have killed to know what Dark Violet whispered in her ear. Whatever it was, they left immediately, the vampire ignoring the rest of her admirers.

I was their shadow as they crossed the street to the Grotto. Dark Violet sailed through the lobby, dinner on her arm.

I catch myself scratching my scar, and stop. Surfing deliciousregre t.com is not helping. Dark Violet's fathomless eyes stare up at me from where she kneels, naked except for the leather and steel accessories she is modeling. I wonder if I looked that good to Preacher, in our Master's dungeon, when he would take me down from the gallery to ... ease his need, and in return, ease mine, helping me fend off insanity.

My hand shakes as I reach for my glass of orange juice. It is all getting old, the headaches, the paranoia, the inability to focus. I can not even distract myself by reading now. This evening I tried to read the same page for twenty minutes and never succeeded. I count off the days in my head, 30. 30 days since my last hunt, 720 hours since being bitten.

Getting up from the table, I wash my breakfast dishes, trying to find some peace in routine, the warm soapy water, the clink of porcelain. I think about the accountant and my mouth twists. She had been so excited. What did she think was going to happen? Was she like me? I had been so eager, hardly believing I had been judged worthy, that I was going to be a vampire. They blindfolded me before taking me stumbling down the steps to that place. When they had put my hands on the table to show me it was there, I leapt up on it, and I thrilled at the fastening of the chains. The vampire introduced herself almost politely, while unseen hands cut my clothes off. Need radiated from her, and for the first time, I felt fear mixed with my elation. Would it hurt? Would she get carried away and devour me completely?

She had pricked me at first, barely puncturing the skin, sending little jabs of pain that made me flinch, but little waves of pleasure, too, that made me squirm. Starting at my neck and working down, she covered me in tiny punctures, licking at each, perhaps getting a little blood. With each prick, my fear and my anticipation grew. Finally, when I thought my heart might burst, she sank her fangs deep into my inner thigh. Agony and ecstasy cruelly intermingled. I had cried out, my back arched, my body rigid, worms of fire crawling through my veins, burrowing agonizing paths to my nipples and my cunt, which felt like they were attached to electrodes. Dimly I heard my own screams. On and on it went, driving all thought from my mind. All that existed was my arched, rigid body, mouth open in an unending howl, and her fangs.

The plate I'm holding slips out of my right hand and splashes into the sink. My left hand is down my pajamas, rubbing my burning thigh. I'm starting to hyperventilate. I grab a paper lunch bag from a drawer and sit on the edge of the bed, breathing into the bag. This can't go on. Soon I'll have to beg Preacher for the relief he used to give me, starting right after the First Bite. I struggled up from darkness, like swimming through tar to reach the surface. My inner thigh was on fire. The bite wound was like a new brand. I was still blindfolded and chained naked to the table, and it was freezing in that basement. Fire and ice, my inner thigh blazing while I shivered from the cold, I felt the Need for the first time. Radiating out from the bite, constricting my veins, making my toes curl and my hands clench into fists. I needed to be bitten. Now. I began to panic. What if she didn't come back for hours or days? I would die from desperation.

There was a clang, like a metal gate closing. Footsteps approached my head. I sensed a swirl of motion above me and almost screamed. A blanket settled over me. Then strong hands lifted my head and held a cup of water to my lips. When I'd finished drinking, those hands removed the blindfold. A figure stood next to the table, towering over me. He had long dark hair, like wings, and eyes that might be blue or might be green. I fell into those eyes like a stone into the sea.

"I have the care of you, until the Master wants you." He scanned my blanket covered form, from head to feet, and back to my face. I trembled like an animal in a trap. "There are ways to ease your suffering.

But you must also ease mine. You can accept my help, and obey me completely, or you can reject it, and the suffering will grow worse." He paused. "Do you want me to help you?"

I swallowed and nodded. He slid his hands under the blanket.

"Starting now, you live to serve."

I did, until the day I struck our Master down.

I catch my breath. Could that be why he warned me to lie low? Does he want me desperate enough to come begging back to him? I shake my head. I can't think that way. That's the paranoia talking. It comes with the shakes and the nausea and all the other trappings of withdrawal. It would be better if I had work tonight. I'm going batshit in this apartment.

***

As I swing up to the Night Fowl's back door on my crutches, I'm encouraged that my ankle hardly hurts. I wondered for a while if it would ever work again, but weeks of pampering have done it a world of good. Good thing, too, because the money Francis gave me is almost gone. I stick my crutches behind the dumpster next to the door. My ankle throbs dully as I put weight on it, but it holds.

I brace myself for the scrutiny I am about to get, and the possibility that the Irregulars have deserted me. Inside, the familiar smell of grease and stale beer makes me smile. I manage to clock in and make it out on the floor without seeing Rob. He had not been happy when I called him about how much work I'd be missing. If I lost Penny's Irregulars, I lost the job, he made clear. Looks like I still have a job.

A quick scan shows Donna, Nicky, Sergio, Tom and Clive in my section. Not bad for being out for so long. Tom spots me first. His eyes go wide like he has seen a ghost. Then he snaps out of it and puts on his salesman's grin. Nicky is sitting with him, and turns to see who Tom is smiling at. She throws both arms up in the air and waves her hands around.

"Penny," she squeals.

The rest spot me now. Donna and Sergio are sharing a plate of nachos, and both stop in the act of feeding their faces. Sergio puts his nacho down and shouts something in Spanish that I can't make out. Donna looks me up and down, assessing. Sitting alone, as always, Clive tips his hat to me.

Wanting a hug from Sergio to help me feel at home, I turn instead to Nicky and Tom's table. If I hug Sergio, they might all want one. Nicky, though, foils my plans and grabs me in a bear hug that threatens to break my spine.

"Penny, Love, where have you been?" She holds me out at arm's length. "We heard you were hurt."

"Rumors of my death were merely wishful thinking," I reply.

"And a sweet dream it was," says Angela, running her words through a cheese grater before delivering them. She approaches with a tray of drinks.

"Your usual, Tom," she says sweetly, putting one in front of him. He thanks her, avoiding my eyes. I think he looks a little pale under his spray-on tan. When he reaches for the drink one of his fingers is splinted and bandaged. I raise an eyebrow.

"Looks like I'm not the only one taking damage."

"Wow, look who noticed someone besides her skinny-ass self."

Nicky takes a step towards Angela, and I can see Angela remember that Nicky almost made it to the Olympics as a boxer, back in the day. I put a hand on Nicky's arm. She tosses her hair and smiles sweetly at Angela.

"You keep up like that, girl, and I'll knock some of those crooked teeth down your throat."

Angela blanches and takes a step back. "Don't touch me, you filthy pervert."

"Ladies, ladies," Sergio interjects, using the term broadly. "Let's all take a deep breath. Angela, now that Penny is here, maybe you should return to the more savory customers in your own section."

Angela looks daggers at him, but he just smiles and sips Tequila.

"Best fucking idea I've heard today." She sashays off.

Nicky sits back down, picks me up by the waist and sits me on her lap.

"Tell Nicky all about it, Honeycomb."

I shrug.

"Missed a step going down the stairs in my building. Twisted my ankle pretty bad. Can't waitress if you can't walk."

"You'd be surprised," Tom says, giving me a blurry smile.

"What's that supposed to mean?"

"Easy, Baby," Nicky says. "He's not being a dick, for a change."

Tom giggles. He must be seriously high. Nicky twists around to talk to Sergio and Donna.

"What about it, you two?" she asks.

Donna finally takes her eyes off me and leans down to pull her giant handbag from under the table. Unzipping it, she pulls out a glass jar with a lid on it. It is stuffed with green, and coins clink as she moves it.

"We collected your tips for you every night you were not here, Chica," says Sergio. The others nod their heads.

I have a lump in my throat all of the sudden. Not only are they still here, but they rallied round. What a bunch of sentimental suckers.

Donna brings the jar and hands it to me. Still sitting on Nicky's lap, I look up at her to say, "Thank you." Before I can, she leans down and kisses me on the forehead, her feverishly hot lips lingering. Suddenly the attention, the physical contact, and the affection are all too much. I jump up off Nicky's lap.

"I've gotta pee," I say, and speed walk to the door to the back, on through and out into the alley. Closing the door on all that humanity, I breathe a little easier. Pressing my back straight against the rough wall of the alley, feeling the bricks through my blouse, my ankle throbs dully.

"Fuck me," I breathe, but smile.

A tremendous "Hrrmph" explodes from the other side of the dumpster, making me jump and magnifying the throbbing in my ankle. Then a voice that has had sandpaper taken to it scolds me.

"That's no way to talk around children."

I push myself away from the wall and limp around the dumpster.

"What children, you crazy old..."

Sitting on the alley floor next to John, are three kids of various sizes and shapes, and one short, gaunt man. They are all wearing clothes that look like they were nice once, but are beginning to get filthy, the way street people's clothes do. They look like bedraggled flowers, long after the bouquet should have been thrown out.

"What are you thinking? This is no place for your children, Pops."

The gaunt man flinches and looks down at his feet. The wave of shame that rolls off him makes my tongue cleave to the top of my mouth. One of the kids, a girl maybe eight or nine, leaps up and stands between her daddy and me, arms stiff at her sides and hands balled into little fists.

"Leave my Daddy alone, Stupidhead."

"Theresa."

"He's a good daddy. You don't know anything. You're just one more meany picking on us 'cause you think we can't do anything about it."

"Theresa."

"You just try being mean to my daddy again and see. I'll bite your fingers off."

"Theresa May Finch, stop that." The girl flies to her father and wraps her arms around his waist, burying her face in his stomach. The two smaller boys look at me with big, solemn eyes.

"This is the nice lady I was telling you about," John says. "Her name is Penny." He looks at me. "Be nice, Little Bird."

I raise an eyebrow at John and motion with my head. He follows me around to the other side of the dumpster.

"What is going on? Why have you been telling them about me, especially lies like I'm nice?"

"He needs a job."

"What?"

"Something to put food in their bellies and a roof over their heads. A better roof than I can find them."

"That has to do with me how?"

"Maybe you can get him a job at the Night Fowl."

"Why are you asking me? I'm just a waitress. Ask Rob."

John scowls. "Rob throws rocks at people like us to get us out of his alley."

Why is this my problem? It is sad, but it is just one more sideshow in this tragicomedy we call life. Then I think of the people back inside the bar, the ones who collected tips for me while putting up with Angela's bullshit. I sigh.

"Why not take them to one of the shelters?"

John steps so close he is almost on top of me. The smell of rotting teeth almost makes me gag, as he breathes into my face.

"Never mention the shelters again. Never. Understand?"

"OK, OK, back off." Crazy old owl.

He takes a step back.

"I know you care, plus," he says, giving me a sly sideways look, "Sunny quit last night."

Fuck me.

No-show graveyard dishwasher is so common, that Rob has authorized me to hire someone off the street and pay them out of petty cash. We don't usually hire them literally off the street, but he has three kids, and I do not want to do the dishes.

I show him the dishwasher setup and the conveyor belt of crap that will bring him his work for the night.

"Do a good job and there might be another night's work for you," I tell him as I hand him the foul rubber apron.

"Thank you. Thank you. If I can just make enough to feed my kids and get cleaned up and some clean clothes again ..."

"Whoa, don't get carried away, Cinderella. Less talking, more cleaning up slop."

"OK, but ..." he moons at me, lunatic hope shining in his eyes.

"But what?"

"My children haven't eaten today."

"For fuck's sake, I hope John doesn't expect to eat tonight." I head for the kitchen to screw up a couple of food orders.

* * *

God. One night back among people and I have had enough. As I reach for the apartment building door, it slams open and a large woman barrels out and into me. We grapple, trying to keep upright, my crutches not helping. She recovers first and manages to step around me, tossing a string of invective back over her shoulder.

Good god damn, once I get back home I am never leaving again. On the way up the steps, I stop to rest twice. Finally, I reach my door. My hand is shaking and I have trouble getting the key in the lock. I lean against the door and use both hands so that I will not shake. Still, it doesn't fit. Kneeling, I examine the lock. It is pristine. No scratches from other nights trying to put the key in. No fingerprint smudges. No history.

What the fuck? I paid the rent on time. They cannot have cause to evict me. I shift my weight and something in the pocket of my jeans pokes me. I didn't have anything in my pockets. From my pocket, I fish out a little manila envelope. How ... Oh shit. That woman at the door. That was no accident. Hurriedly I check the contents of my little purse. Everything is there, tips and all.

I tip the contents of the envelope into the palm of my hand. A key. God, oh god no, not in my own home. Please. The key fits perfectly in the lock, and turns soundlessly. I take several slow, deep breaths before I stand and throw the door open.

He is sitting in one of my kitchen chairs, facing the door. I have never seen the Vampire Mayor, but I can tell it is him by the way I step across the threshold and drop to my knees, my eyes locked to his. He has razor blades for eyes.

"Close the door, Penny."

His voice is the sound of hammers raining on sheet metal. My First Bite burns like a branding iron is being pressed to my inner thigh. Shuffling forward on my knees, I close the door, never taking my eyes off his. He snaps his fingers and points to the floor next to him.

I put my hands on the floor and crawl. It is all I can do not to slither to him on my belly. I am shaking, and the closer I get to him, nausea begins to roil in my stomach. When I reach him, I nuzzle his pants with my cheek. He rests his hand on the back of my head, twining his fingers in my hair.

"You've been a bad girl, Penny. Killing my ambassador. Murdering who knows how many of my constituents. Regular little Jack the Ripper you are."

He fists his hand in my hair and pulls my head back until it feels like my neck might snap, forcing me to look at him.

"Lucky for you, I have a use for bad girls." He lets go of my hair and my head snaps forward, almost hitting the floor. I pant, and wait.

"Vampires are an unruly lot, Penny. We chafe at authority. Yet to survive the humans, we must have order. I can always use a good assassin. A viper to loose in the house of mine enemies."

He wants me to kill vampires for him?

"How ... how did you find me?"

He chuckles. "It was not hard, once I knew to look for you. I know a lot of people, and everyone is connected to someone."

Oh, Preacher, I'm sorry ...

"But you mustn't blame Tom, my dear. It was the threat against his niece and nephew that pried it loose. He doesn't seem the type, does he, but those children mean the world to him."

"Tom?"

"Very different from, what was his name, Francis? He said his family didn't know he existed, so why betray a friend for them."

My throat tightens.

"It was mostly screaming after that. And begging." He pets my hair. "I especially love the begging."

A new emotion riots inside me, one I have never truly felt before. Hate. Tossing my head, I throw his hand off and sit back on my heels. Preparing to stand, I glare at him, and his eyes cut into mine. I find myself on my hands and knees again. Pain flares in my thigh, sending worms of fire wriggling into my veins. My sobs turn into moans. My need is so big it leaves no room to hate him, or myself.

"Please," I whimper.

He laughs, and each peal of glee is a dagger stabbing my eardrums.

"Oh, you are a find, Bad Penny."

Casually, he backhands me, flinging me sideways and sending me rolling until I hit the wall.

"That is all the satisfaction you are going to get from me, today." He stands. "Do not contact me, my office will contact you."

I watch his workman's boots cross the floor. He stops at the door.

"Welcome to the administration," he says, then leaves, closing the door behind him.

I curl up into a ball. My face is starting to hurt, but that discomfort is dwarfed by the burning. It lessened slightly when he hit me, but flares worse than ever when he leaves. I am not going to be able to take this. With no vampire lined up for seduction, I have one choice.

I crawl to where my purse landed when the Vampire Asshole knocked me across the room. Dialing the number I know best, I hold my breath. After the third ring ...

"Talk."

"The Mayor was here. He didn't hurt me ... much."

There is silence, then a low growl.

"Preacher, he didn't hurt me ... right."

Another silence.

"Penny, I don't think ..."

"Don't think, just come. Please. I need you."

I hear a long, slow breath.

"Do you remember the rules?"

"I remember everything."

"Are you certain, Penny?"

"I'm begging."

"You know how I want to find you. Do not disappoint me."

"No, Sir. I won't. I will be your good girl."

I gasp at the fire worms wriggling in my veins. His breathing quickens, and he hangs up.

***

Giving me time to shower and prepare myself, he knocks on the door an hour later.

"It is open, Sir. Please come in, Sir."

He opens the door, pauses, then steps in and closes it behind him. I kowtow, arms stretched in front of me, forehead resting on the floor, wearing only a collar.

"Up."

I rise onto my knees, clasp my hands behind my head, and push my chest forward. I have written, "Use Me," across my breasts, with one arrow pointing up, and one arrow pointing down, in black marker. He smiles a hungry smile.

"Do you remember our safe word?"

"Ecclesiastes."

"Good. Now crawl to the shower."

"I bathed just before you arrived, Sir."

"Crawl to the shower."

I crawl. He walks close behind me, and I can feel him staring. Can he see how wet I am? I blush from head to toe.

"You are going to bathe me. Then I am going to treat you the way you need to be treated."

I do, and he does.

Afterward, he wraps me in two thick bath towels and holds me in his lap. I rest my head on his chest. The fire in my veins is muted to a warm tingling, and my First Bite is a dull ache.

"Thank you," I murmur.

"How are you," he asks, his voice deep and mellow.

"Ummm, so much better."

"But you still need to be bitten."

I shrug.

"It'll take a while to get bad again. Gives me time to find a victim."

He traces my jaw with a finger. I turn my head so I can suck on it.

"The Mayor was here?"

A little tension comes back between my shoulders.

"Let's not talk about it yet."

I drift off to sleep in his arms.

***

"I will have to kill him."

Banging my tea down on the table hard enough to splash my hand, I jerk it away.

"Ow!"

He looks at me steadily with those two chunks of burning sea he calls eyes.

"Are you crazy?" I demand.

"No, but I protect my own." He smiles one of his thin, humorless smiles. "Even when it is not wise. The entire side of your face is bruised. It was him?"

I nod. Preacher growls in the back of his throat. I look down into my tea.

"He did worse." I swallow hard.

"Penny?"

"He killed a friend of mine, and his family, to get to me."

The first tears well up in my eyes. Before, horror and need had dammed them up, but now I'm safe and relaxed. Now the tears come. Poor Francis.

Preacher covers my hand with his.

"I will paint the walls of his office with his blood."

I sniffle.

"Can you take him?"

"I've wanted to find out for a long time."

"Can you take them all? Every last vampire in this town? Because a human kills their mayor, they can't let that human live. Even if they wanted the mayor dead themselves."

"It won't happen that way."

"Bullshit. You'll be dead, and then where will I be?"

"It won't ..."

"Yes, it will. If you kill the Vampire Mayor, I will never talk to you again."

He leans back in his chair and chuckles. "Because I'll be dead."

"I don't see what's funny about it."

He holds up his hands as if to ward me off.

"OK, Penny, OK." He puts his hands down. "What are you going to do?"

"Work for him."

***

Another tryst with Dusk is just ending, orange light quickly fading from the walls and my skin when the phone rings. I smile. Preacher is the only person who calls me. Even my boss at the Night Fowl only has the number of the answering service I use. I've fought my attraction to Preacher for so long because I did not want to be a slave again, but this time I realize he needs me at least as much as I need him. He's calling me, after all. God it would be nice to have someone take care of me just a little.

I pick up the phone and purr, "Good timing, I haven't put clothes on yet."

"We have a strict, 'No shirt, No shoes, No service,' policy at the Mayor's office, but I have always noted that it does not specify pants, so make of that what you will."

The voice is female and the diction is clipped and precise, like a gardener using sheers.

"Your appointment is at 10 PM sharp. That is when the Mayor will see you. You will have enrollment paperwork, so get here by 9:30 PM at the latest. Bring two forms of ID, one government with your picture on it. The names on the ID's do not have to match, but the addresses do. We understand some of our employees have a need for misdirection."

There is a patient pause before I blurt out, "There's paperwork?"

"Glad you are keeping up. I will now tell you the address of the Mayor's office. I will repeat it as many times as it takes you to memorize it. You will not write it down. Ready?"

***

I look for street numbers on the row of seemingly identical, abandoned warehouses. It's difficult because only half the street lights work. They all have faded, peeling paint and broken windows. If you pay attention, a few show signs of use, a collection of cigarette butts and Styrofoam cups around a battered folding chair at the mouth of an alley, a too shiny deadbolt on one of the rusted front doors. Only one has the street number freshly painted on the curb in front. I don't need the number to know I am at my destination. My First Bite started to itch as soon as I was in front of the building.

The front door hinges squeal like a banshee. The first floor is dark and silent and smells of dust and mildew. "Vamp Mayor is old school," I mutter. I slip through the shadows towards the lone bare bulb that makes a forlorn pool of light deep inside the warehouse. As the woman had told me, it illuminates the bottom of a flight of stairs. The steel treads vibrate slightly under my feet as I climb to a catwalk two or three stories above the floor. Turning left as I had been instructed, I trail my hand along the wall until I feel a doorway. I open the door into a small room dimly illuminated by light from under yet another door. My First Bite is burning like a brand on my inner thigh. I knock once and enter. I am immediately blinded by the bright light.

"That's not an accidental effect," I say out loud.

The voice from the phone orders, "Close the door behind you, please."

As my eyes adjust, I see I'm in a moderately sized room, paneled in rich, dark wood. There is a collection of brown leather club chairs scattered here and there, but the room is dominated by a huge wood desk right out of some office furniture porn mag. Perched behind it, in almost a caricature of perfect posture, is the woman I had seen leaving the Dome Room with Dark Violet.

"I thought you were an accountant," I blurt out.

The woman frowns almost imperceptibly. "Do accountants normally call people to make appointments for their employer?"

"No, of course not. Silly me."

"Do not do that."

"What?"

"Play dumb." She extends her arm, a clipboard in her hand. "This is your paperwork. Please have a seat and fill it out. The Mayor will see you promptly at ten."

Her desk is so big we both have to lean forward for the hand-off. The top two buttons of her blouse are unbuttoned, and the glimpse of cleavage makes my burning thigh flare even more. There's a hitch in my breathing and I steady myself with my free hand. Without looking to see if the woman has noticed, I hurry to one of the club chairs. When I sit I cross my legs so that I can rub them one against the other. The words on the form swim before my eyes for a moment, then slowly come into focus.

"You want my social security number?"

"It is customary for employment."

"Bank account and routing number?"

"For direct deposit. Pages two and three are medical, page four is dental. I am afraid the Administration does not provide vision." She touches her own, old-fashioned glasses.

My tongue involuntarily probes the molar that's been hurting since I dropped two stories onto a vampire gangster. Then I see the figure next to salary and let out a low whistle.

"You have come to the salary. The Administration values its employees. You are in one of the higher brackets because your position is subject to higher than normal risk."

There is something in her voice that might be pride.

"I developed the tables used for determining salary."

"See, Accountant."

She almost smiles.

I barely have time to fill out the forms by the time the clock says ten. I'm sure the woman will disapprove of my handwriting but don't have time to worry about it for long before the door to the Vampire Mayor's office opens and his deep voice rumbles into the waiting room.

"Come in, Penny."

I do not remember dropping to my hands and knees or crawling across the room. I simply find myself kneeling in front of the vampire, who is leaning against his desk, ankles crossed.

"Goodness, me. It's a testament to the iron will that makes me Mayor, that I don't devour you right now."

"Wouldn't that be, badness you?" I gasp out. He chuckles.

"Oh, you are one to talk, my very, very bad Penny. I suspect that's part of your lethality to vampires. You are the bait for your own traps, aren't you?"

I nod, biting my tongue to stop myself from whimpering.

"How do you kill us?"

"Trade secret," I spit out and then clamp my teeth back down on my tongue.

He regards me silently for a moment. I am unable to look away from his razor blade eyes.

"Most vampires, younger vampires, would force you to tell. I understand that sometimes mysteries are delicate. If you told me your secret, Penny, would it take away your ability to kill us?"

I nod.

"Well, we don't want that." His manner turns brusque and he moves to behind his desk and sits. "Stand up, Penny. Show some dignity."

I get shakily to my feet.

"My administration has been good for vampires. The food supply is stable and vampire fatalities are low and predictable, with a few exceptions." He nods at me. "This is not the norm for vampires. Our history is one of being hunted, of living on the edge of starvation, except for a few lucky ones who manage to have long lives of luxury, the vampire one percent."

"So, what, you're looking out for the working class vampire by cozying up to the mob?"

"Ah, that little problem you caused me that brought you to my attention. Our Italian friends are quite upset about that."

"You pay humans for protection, is that it? Is that the covenant I've heard about? Seems a little like groveling before humans, doesn't it?"

"The Covenant is not some protection racket. We work with the other powers instead of fighting them. What I've achieved for us in this city is extraordinary, but vampires, Penny, vampires are not good followers, and the myth of the vampire aristocrat, living in opulence and bathing themselves in blood is a hard dream to kill. Some of my constituents chafe under my administration's regulations on their appetite. Believe it or not, they seek to undermine our achievements, even bring down my administration."

He pauses as if he expects me to reply, but I am only getting about half of what he says. It's all I can do to stay on my feet. He frowns, then continues.

"Fine, I'll get to the point. There is a resistance. You will kill their leader." He shoves a folder across his desk. "This is a dossier on your target."

I pick up the folder, but do not open it. Worms of fire crawl through my veins, emanating from my First Bite. Nausea roils in my gut.

"I almost forgot." He reaches into a desk drawer and retrieves a business card, which he hands to me. "I want the body as proof you have completed the task. Call this number and tell them where it is."

I look at the card and frown. "Detective Rose Romero?"

"She'll take care of it. Just tell her where you leave the corpse."

"You work with the other powers. Do you mean the cops are involved, too?"

"You think too small. A leader like myself makes deals with other leaders, not lackeys. Now I grow tired of this meeting. Go."

"Please," I whimper.

He raises an eyebrow, then stands and moves around the desk to stand next to me. "Please what?"

"Please bite me." I admire myself for the way I beg this monster.

He leans in close, his hot breath on my neck. My heart is trying to pound its way out of my chest, and my entire body trembles.

"Not today," he whispers in my ear.

Once again, I do not remember crossing the room. When I cross the threshold into the waiting room, the door slams behind me. I drop to my hands and knees and puke up my meager breakfast. The secretary lifts my face by my chin and wipes off the filth around my mouth.

"You are the worst case I have seen."

***

I sip my coffee and watch Preacher eat. He throws huge forkfuls of grits and runny eggs into his mouth like he hasn't eaten for days. His appetites are always like that. We are in our old booth at Mollie's. I called him as soon as I was out of the Vamp district, in bad shape. He took me home and ... took care of me. He was hungry, after, and scolded me for not having any food in the place. So he brought me to Mollie's just before dawn.

I feel displaced in time. How many times have we been here togeth-er, a thousand? They all run together, like an endless impressionistic breakfast, the same smells of frying food and unwashed bodies, and Preacher's particular scent, heavy male musk tinged with something sharp and clean. The same clinking of silverware on chipped plates, and the endless slurping of coffee from the giant, steaming pots. I barely resist the old habit of sliding under the table and waiting on my knees. Life was so much simpler then, after we'd struck down our mistress and gone out on our own. I hadn't been ready to return to the world. Instead, I embraced a new master, no worries other than his pleasure, no bills, no time card, no appointments, no planning for the future. I took care of his needs, and he took care of everything, including the cravings. I lean back against the cool vinyl of the booth and sigh. He looks up at me with those two pieces of burning sea he calls eyes.

"Eat your toast, it will help settle your stomach."

"Oh, you settled my stomach." I stretch languidly. "Reset my whole body to optimal."

"Eat your toast and tell me again."

I take a bite of toast, soggy with butter.

"There isn't much. He has a ... problem he wants me to take care of. Did I mention I get dental insurance?"

"You need to take this seriously. She is not your usual prey."

"Why didn't you tell me about the Covenant? You obviously know about it. Don't you think you should share something like that?"

"It is dangerous information, and I only have a partial picture. I will help you with this kill."

I shake my head. "After, not before. You're too conspicuous. Every vampire in this town knows the man who slew his mistress and took her menagerie for his own."

He looks down at his plate. "Only it was your hand ..."

"How many of them do you still have?" I interrupt.

He meets my eyes again. "Three. The rest are independent or ..." He shrugs, an odd expression of helplessness from such a man.

"Or they found a new set of fangs."

"If they survive long enough I reclaim them." He clenches his fists on the gouged Formica table. "But some have not."

I lean forward and rest my hands on his fists. "You have saved some of the unsavable."

His big hands relax under mine. "And they have saved me."

"How many vampires have you killed to protect your girls?"

"I rival you."

"I thought so."

"But I did not kill the first one."

In my mind, I see the flickering movie that is my memory of that dawn when Preacher freed me from my chains while the Mistress was sleeping and vulnerable. I feel the heft of the axe he had given me, its surprising weight as I swung it over my head.

"No, you didn't." I pause for a heartbeat. "How did she choose?"

"What?"

"I have never asked you, how did she choose her prey?"

He pales and pulls his hands from under mine. He is silent.

"You chose us for her, didn't you? It was one of your jobs that you did oh so well."

He nods, his eyes never leaving mine.

"I always knew, I think. Not that I had to be captured or anything, I was so eager. Is that why you picked me?"

His eyes really are as wide as oceans now, and I think he trembles.

"Once having seen you, I could no more not choose you than I could stop breathing."

I slide around the booth so I'm next to him and brush the hair from his feverish brow, kissing his forehead. "I forgive you."

He rests his head on my shoulder and breathes in deep, ragged breaths.

"I will need your help after. I have a plan for the body."

"And the approach?"

"Oh, you are going to hate this."

***

I expected The Grounded to be brown leather armchairs and an assortment of World Beat CD's on sale at the counter. What I find are overly used couches and photocopied fliers for local bands. I try to smile at the young woman who makes my Cappuccino, but the Patchouli wafting off her is like a spike in my eye.

Taking a seat at a small table in a corner, I do a threat assessment of my fellow patrons, looking for bite marks or clues they also do not belong. This table is equidistant from the front door and the opening of the narrow hallway with the "Fire Exit" sign above it. My hands are barely shaking. He's part of city government, and the Vampire Mayor implied he has a deal with the human Mayor. Does the Pretender know about the vampires and humans? I'm counting on it.

The Pretender is exactly one minute early. He comes straight to my table.

"Miss Penny, what a treat. But I had been hoping I'd beat you here and I could treat you." He has an honest-to-god twinkle in his eye, and his voice is warm and welcoming.

"You mean you assumed I would be late," I growl.

He laughs. "No offense intended. I assumed you were not a morning person, and might find this hour difficult."

"It was morning the first time we met."

"Point to you. I apologize." He points over his shoulder with his thumb. "Let me get some coffee and then we'll see if I can do better."

I watch him stroll to the counter. He does not swagger, yet there is an air of quiet confidence about him. The hippie chick Barista warms to him instantly, launching into customary banter with a favorite regular. He's on his home turf, which is what I wanted. He will be less on his guard.

"Are you hungry? They do an edible breakfast burrito."

"I'll pass."

"You can have some of mine when they bring it. If you change your mind."

All charm. Now he'll ask me why I called him. He leans forward, elbows on the table.

"Have you read any Darcy Higgins?"

I blink at him. He continues.

"I'm reading her next to latest, A Pearl In Search of An Oyster. Utterly fascinating. The concepts about origin stories and parentage she's exploring are blowing my mind."

"No, I haven't read any of her yet. But I have her first book, The Back of My Hand, on hold at the library."

"Ha! One of my guesses proves true. You're a book person."

"Not as much as I used to be, but I'm starting to use the library again. The online search and hold makes it a whole new thing."

"I know. You can browse the whole county's catalog, put a hold on what you want, even if it's on the shelf, then breeze in, pick it up, and breeze out. It's a completely different experience than going in and hunting for what you want."

We talk books. Old favorites, new finds, books that changed the way we saw the world. Books that were the most possible fun you could find sandwiched between two pieces of cardboard. Easily an hour has passed before I find my way back to my mission.

"Do you want to know why I asked you here?"

"Only if it is frivolous or funny."

"I want you to help me kill a vampire."

He slaps the table and grins at me. "That qualifies."

"What's funny about it?"

"You're not serious?"

"I am."

He sits very still and watches me for a long moment.

"You do know that they are real, right? Or are you one of the clueless?"

Now he can impress me with his role in the government, his secret knowledge of the Covenant, be the big man.

He smiles, and it is the first time I've seen him smile without warmth.

"You are not going to manipulate me by making me feel uncool, Penny."

Damn, I'm screwing this up.

"The monsters in the dark are real, and I hunt them. Do you want in?"

"First you try to make me feel uncool, then you offer me a chance to be the ultra-cool Vampire Hunter. It's not working. I was having fun, but now you are wasting my time."

Great. I've insulted him. Should have just slept with him and then led him around by his cock.

"That's pathetic, too, Penny."

"What?"

"Your playbook is obvious. You are thinking Plan B, right, which is suggest you'll fuck me if I help you? I am not flattered by the way you underestimate me."

I push my chair back and stand.

"Then I should stop wasting your time."

He smiles up at me, warmth seeping back in. "That's better. I came down here and spent real time with you, so I'm interested. Sit back down and try again."

I sit down and think about it. Really think about it.

"Would you like to know what makes me tick?" I lean across the table and make the most intense eye contact I can. "Do you want to know what my obsession is? My addiction that I order my whole life around? Maybe get an inkling of why I'm hooked so hard?"

He leans across the table until our faces are very close. "Yes."

***

Dark Violet is pure kinetic magic on stage. A wall of sound with a slow, heavy beat is her backdrop. She is the cobra in the snake charmer's dance, and she is the charmer. Ripples and undulations promise delicious friction, should you try to contain her in your arms, and the occasional striking motion she makes with her head makes my knees go weak.

My scar feels like army ants crawling up my thigh. Veins constricted, mouth dry, I would have already climbed on stage and offered myself to her, if not for the Pretender's hand on my shoulder.

It's a simple plan. Get near her and let her feel the hunger, pander to her tastes. My hair is back in a severe bun, and my spotless white button down, black pencil skirt, and pantyhose are impeccable, or were before joining this heaving, sweaty mass of humanity at the dark goddess's feet.

We are near the stage, and I have caught her eye once or twice. It's time to move to our next position. I try to turn my head to speak to the Pretender, but I can't, and my tongue is stuck to the top of my mouth so that I cannot ask for help. He must sense my distress, because he moves to stand between me and the stage, cutting off my view.

"Is it time to move, do you think?" he asks.

I give him a grateful little nod. He is wearing round, blue tinted sunglasses, despite the dimness of the club. When I asked why, he had just shrugged, and handed me a ring, which he told me to put on my right hand. It was about the size of a class ring and had three interlocking circles engraved on it. Again, no explanation. I had done as I was told.

We turn away from the stage and strike out towards the edge of the crowd. The Pretender has to push, squeeze and apologize. I slip through the gaps between bodies like sand through a sieve. The music cuts off abruptly, then kicks off again with a new song and a faster tempo. Dark Violet stage dives into the crowd without hesitation or warning, caught by dozens of eager hands, which begin passing her away from the stage. This isn't part of the plan. What vampire would toss themselves into a crowd of humans, the predator making themselves vulnerable to a mob of prey?

She's almost halfway to the edge of the crowd and I'm beginning to panic. If the plan fails, I am no closer to relief. Several pairs of hands holding up Dark Violet suddenly disappear. The crowd nearly drops her, then recovers enough to set her gently on her feet. Without looking around, Dark Violet begins cutting through the throng towards her table of wannabes.

Intercepting her at the edge of the crowd, I trip and stumble into the vampire. She tries to brush me aside with an arm that feels like an iron bar, but I cling to her to keep from falling. She stops, disgust rolling off of her in waves. I look up into her face, eyes wide, lips parted, and breathing rapidly.

"I'm ... so ... sorry," I stutter, and swallow hard. The hard, angular lines of her face frame eyes that are whirlpools of darkness. They draw me to press my entire body against the length of her. Her lips curve slightly, and I feel an arm slip around my waist, slowly crushing me against her with inexorable strength. The words, "Take me," start to form on my lips, when someone starts shouting in my ear.

"Are you OK, Penny? I saw you trip."

Dark Violet looks at the Pretender before I do, breaking eye contact, her mouth becoming a hard, thin line.

"Thank you for catching her."

"Go away, Philip," she says, each word a bullet.

"No, Violet. She's mine."

She grabs my right arm and yanks my hand up in front of her face, then snarls when she sees the ring on my finger. Shooting the Pretender a venomous glance, she lets go of me. Shuddering, I take a step back. The vampire steps close to the Pretender, and I feel a whisper of vampire magic. She stares straight into those weird sunglasses.

"You dare bring her to my hunting ground? You are a fool to bait me."

He is pale but stands his ground. That's wrong. He should be mesmerized, the vampire filling up his whole world.

"There are no hunting grounds allowed under the Covenant, as you well know. This is neutral ground."

"What is allowed and what is true are not always the same."

The Pretender shrugs. "Nonetheless, she is with me."

Her lips pull back in a snarl, revealing her fangs, right in public Without taking her eyes from his face, she waves a hand. One of her wannabes rushes forward.

"An invitation, Janice, for my new friend."

Janice scurries to the wannabe table, and back. She hands something to Dark Violet, who holds it out to me. It is a shiny heart, anatomically correct, with a bite taken out of it.

"I'm having a very exclusive party Thursday night. You are invited." I reach out and take it. "Leave that awful ring at home," she adds. Without looking at the Pretender again, she sweeps away towards her table, the girl Janice following in her wake.

The Pretender looks pale and serious. Taking my arm proprietarily, he steers me to the door and out into the relative cool and calm of the street. He keeps quiet as we put one foot in front of the other, giving the night room to be.

"You knew her."

"I know a lot of people."

"She's not people."

He pushes the glasses up on his forehead and gives me his brilliant smile.

"My job brings me into contact with all kinds. I better have the ring back now."

I take the ring off my finger and hand it to him. He slips it into his pocket.

"I'm not going to even ask about that."

That smile again. "I knew you were a smart girl."

"Thanks for coming. Your timing was perfect, plus breaking up the crowd surfing so I could run into her. I couldn't have done it without you."

"Did you get what you wanted?"

I hold up the invitation.

"Yep."

***

The trap is set. Now to become the bait. Always keeping her prey selection in mind, I'm going for sexed-up accountant. Fitted white button down, tucked into the top of my black wiggle skirt. The skirt fits snugly, hugging my hips and forming a tight cone to just below my knees. I am wearing black heels that say, "Fuck me," more than, "Let me do your taxes." My hair is back in a severe bun that makes my scalp feel tight, and I'm wearing a minimum of makeup. Searching my prop box, I finally find the black-framed glasses that are the final touch.

Dark Violet is no drooling adolescent. She's been around and is unlikely to go for anyone too eager, or obviously vulnerable. What I am presenting is a woman who travels this life on strict and narrow paths, yet has accepted an invitation to a party completely off her map. A woman who dresses like a proper professional woman should, except for those too high heels. A woman who accepts that she is to be feminine and on display, that her appearance is of utmost importance, but that she is for looking at, not touching. Except maybe that is starting to slip. Perhaps with just the right pressure applied at precisely the right point, well, who knows what a woman like that might do.

That woman in the mirror gives me a nervous smile, eyes a little wild. The bait is ready.

Removing the Caravaggio print from the wall, I dial the combination of the safe, a mash-up of my mother's birthday and my high school best friend's phone number. I open the safe to the smell of leather and antiseptic. Taking the Doctor's bag to the table, I spread out its contents, checking each piece. Satisfied, I take the aluminum tube and slip it into my little black purse, then put the rest back in the bag. It is a moment's work to close the safe and return the painting. The last step is to grab a bag of plasma from the fridge. I text, "Game on," to the number I know best, as I leave my building. I hope I left early enough to catch the midnight train. No way I can run in these heels.

***

The blue line rushes past the lights of uptown, murmuring to itself and rocking back and forth. Sweating, gray faced men and women, pressed shoulder to shoulder, avoid each other's eyes while trying to catch glimpses through curtained windows of families at dinner, lovers entangled, scenes from their favorite syndicated sitcoms, all transmuted into a silent montage of heartbreaking beauty. I am sitting on my hands to keep from scratching my scar bloody.

The small man in an overlarge T-shirt and dirty baseball cap sitting next to me is perched on the edge of the seat, leaving maximum space between us. A rare gentleman in a fallen age. I feel a huge fondness for him. I consider sliding closer to him, letting him know it is OK if his shoulder bumps me, or his thigh presses against mine, but he wouldn't appreciate it. He would be disappointed I wasn't a lady worthy of his gallantry. I am sad when he gets off at the Elm stop.

A suit with CEO hair wins the contest for the free seat. He smells strongly of musk and money, and his elbow brushes mine. Giving me what he thinks is a wolfish grin, he says, "Now that's a nice change, isn't it?"

I lean close to his clean-shaven cheek and whisper, "Can I show you something," and then lean away. He raises an eyebrow.

"This is a little public, but I'm game."

I unzip the doctor's bag on my lap, put my hand in, and motion him to lean over and look in. As he does, I whip out a scalpel and hold it next to his nose.

"I could cut the tip off before you could flinch."

The swaying of the train moves his face further from and closer to the blade. Wide-eyed, he doesn't speak. I hear a grunt from the seat behind me. Can't do this for long without causing a commotion. I pull the scalpel away from his face and rest that hand on top of my bag.

"Go."

He's on his feet and shoving his way through the crowded aisle, followed by loud complaints. This time it's a chuckle that I hear behind me. A polite, "Excuse me," is followed by a man climbing over the back of the seat to sit next to me.

"You have a gift for trouble," says Preacher.

"It's what I do best."

I put the scalpel back in the bag, zip it, and hand it to him.

"Repeat the plan to me," I say.

He gives me a half-smile I read as bemused.

"This morning I checked into the Groto under a false name. Paid for one night, in advance, cash. You owe me $200." I wince. "I had luggage, a large trunk on rollers. Left it in my room, #423. I went on with my day. That brings us to this evening. We meet on the Blue

Line, Chandler stop, at midnight. You bring the bag, I come empty handed. I get off one stop ahead of you, with the bag, and take my time returning to the room at the Grotto, where I wait for your call."

I nod. "What are you going to do while you wait?"

He pats his shirt pocket, and I hear the crinkle of paper.

"Meditation on the Book of Ecclesiastes."

The train brakes and he looks up. "My stop," he says. He rises and exits the train, taking the bag with him.

I should bail. Ride right past the Grotto stop, get off at the next platform, and switch to the Northbound. Go home. But the memory of that arm like an iron bar crushing me against her whip-lean body comes crashing through my good sense. My scar prickles like pins are being stuck down its whole length. I look around at these gray cipher people on the train, with their gray lives, with their stale problems and zombie triumphs. My mouth tastes like rotting flesh and I start to gag.

Closing my eyes, I summon the first bite, the agony and ecstasy fusing me into a single piece of white-hot glass. The nausea recedes. In my mind, Preacher punishes me for breaking the rules of whatever game we are playing to keep the shadows away, knowing I'd broken them on purpose. Looking into the future, I am wrapped around Dark Violet as if I am trying to absorb her, her fangs buried in my throat, our hearts beating in time.

The train brakes. My stop. Time to party.

The Grotto's green and gold stained glass doors open and close briskly. The lobby is well populated for a weeknight. Groups of two and three are scattered among the overstuffed chairs, here two elderly sisters traveling together, there a couple doing their best Bogey and Bacall. There are a few families, smaller children sleeping on their parent's laps, older children sipping Shirley Temples from the bar, wide-eyed at being up this late. I approach the concierge behind her desk of dark wood. She looks up at my approach, expression neutral.

"Can I help you?"

"Could you point me to Conference Room E?"

"Are you sure you have the right room? What event are you here for?"

"This is the invitation," I say, pulling it from my little black purse.

She glances at it, then pushes her chair back, stands, and walks briskly around her desk. Standing as close to me as she can without touching me, she puts her mouth close to my ear and says quietly, "We have a no corpse cleanup policy at the Grotto. Observe it."

She steps back from me and says in a louder voice, "Staircase B will take you down one floor. Turn right at the bottom of the stairs, third door on your left." She points behind me as she speaks.

I turn and look for Staircase B. The sign is spelled out in ornate bronze letters over a door directly behind me. My heels click on the marble as I walk dazedly in that direction. What was she warning me about, becoming a corpse, or making one?

11

DARK VIOLET

Dark Violet knows the moment her quarry enters the room. After all these hundreds of years, she still does not know exactly how. Scent is certainly part of it, but not all. A human being has a certain energy, like an electrostatic cloud around them that interacts with every object or person they come near. Humans sense it, but dully. They call it aura, or put it down to pheromones. Violet believes her skin is one big antenna, covered in special receptors for recognizing prey. When she identifies a new partner in the dance of death, she becomes attuned to them, so that their presence is no longer a breeze on the back of the neck, but a crashing wave. When Penny plunges into the throng of partygoers, her energy ripples through the room like a bomb going off.

She's searching the crowd. Violet knows the search is for her, and eludes the woman. Letting the excitement and desperation grow is like marinating a steak. Violet lets Penny get almost close enough to call out to her and then disappears into the swirl of the crowd. Now the vampire waits until the prey catches sight of her again, then grabs a beautiful boy by the hair and kisses him savagely. She can feel her prey's heart beat even faster, nearly panicking at the prospect of being passed over for another. The Vamp's own hunger begins to rise like a tide.

She lets her pursuer catch her, drinking champagne by the tinkling fountain.

"I didn't expect you to play hard to get," the woman says.

Violet raises an eyebrow. Usually, they are begging by this point. The woman's pulse is fast, and she is sweating profusely, her animal smell making Violet's nose twitch, but she has her wits about her.

"Why would you expect anything of me," asks Violet.

"Coy doesn't really suit a magnificent monster like you."

The vampire takes in the tight black skirt and severe button-down, a costume meant for her. She reaches out and brushes the woman's long hair away from her neck, feeling for the faint puncture scars.

"Oh, you are bad, Penny," she sighs.

This one is trouble. She will not be a keeper, but a one time indulgence. Violet can let her appetite have free reign.

"To my room, then."

***

She leads Penny into the center of the hotel room, the door closing behind them with a discreet click.

"Stand here. Do not move from this spot."

From a drawer by the bed, she retrieves a collar with a steel ring in it. She holds it out to the woman. Penny takes it without hesitation and puts it on without fumbling. Violet stands very, very close to the woman, feeling her vibrate.

"Undress. No, slowly." Violet circles her as Penny struggles to slow herself down, tracing invisible lines of desire on the trembling flesh as it is uncovered. This is the beautiful dance. Violet's kind call it hunting, but why chase and rend when they would give themselves to you, trembling with lust and self-destruction? Their need for release, for annihilation is so big for such fragile creatures. Violet stands before this one now, staring into her hot eyes, caressing a hip, twisting a nipple. The beauty of this body, this pathetic, lovely woman is hers for the taking. It is her great privilege to give them what they need, and their great gift to be devoured. She shivers from head to toe.

"We will start with a bath."

12

BAD PENNY

The Good Doctor rushes into the antechamber, despite having kicked me out last visit. She stops abruptly when she sees us. I had had Preacher wait outside the view of her camera at the door, so he and our cargo were a surprise. I can't help admire how quickly she recovers, haughtiness covering that brief glimpse of surprise, and perhaps a glimmer of fear.

"You have brought me a coffin and a Preacher. Is this your addled idea of a prank?"

I look up at Preacher, who I am leaning heavily against, and say, "Told you everyone knows you."

The fatigue of being drained by Dark Violet tries to drag me down into unconsciousness, but I pull myself up straight.

"This is not a prank, it is a delivery." I put my hand on the coffin bungeed to the upright dolly. Excitement lights up her face, another first.

"You have brought me a live specimen?", she demands.

"There are no living vampires, and you are a fool to ask for such a thing," Preacher replies, in a flat, disapproving tone.

"Then what are you playing at with this," the Good Doctor sneers.

Time for me to take back control of the conversation. "It's the next best thing, or rather the best thing, since like Preacher said, you are nuts to ask for a living ..."

"...animated..." Preacher interjects.

"...animated vamp," I finish.

Preacher tilts the dolly back at a seventy degree angle, while I begin to remove the bungee cords. My hands are shaking and I talk to cover my weakness.

"All you've ever had before were pieces and parts." I wrestle the lid of the coffin off. Inside is the naked and utterly still corpse of Dark Violet. My breath catches in my chest for a moment at her beauty. "My latest, and most magnificent victim, completely whole and all for you."

The Good Doctor makes a sound between a gasp and a moan. I wrench my gaze away from the spectacular contents of the coffin and try to nail her with my gaze.

"At a price." It comes out as barely above a whisper. I'm fading fast.

The Good Doctor doesn't look away from the prize. "I see no justification for changing the terms of our agreement. You acquired it with means I provided. It belongs to me."

"You bitch..." I try to take a step towards her but stumble and grab onto the coffin for support.

"Possession is nine tenths of the law," Preacher says, threats bobbing just beneath the surface of his words.

"You should be a great supporter of my work," she replies to him. "You understand that I'm more responsible for these vampire deaths than she is?"

He shrugs. "You will give her what she asks for, or I will dump this in the river."

"Then she'll do no more business with me."

"Which you already threatened her with. You can both have what you want. That's the nature of a bargain."

The Good Doctor actually smiles. I shiver.

"So it is," she says. "Wait here."

I slide down into the chair, shivering and trying to keep my teeth from chattering. Preacher puts the lid of the coffin back and puts the bungees back on. The Good Doctor returns, carrying two aluminum test tubes.

"It will be useful if you leave the dolly."

Preacher nods agreement and takes the two tubes, one in each hand, comparing their weight. "It would be unwise to cheat her."

That creepy smile appears on her face again.

"Penny is lucky to have you as a ..."

"Associate," Preacher interrupts.

She looks at me now, her expression changing.

"Now get her out of my waiting room."

13

BAD PENNY

I slowly surface, not so much from sleep, but from murky dreams of suicide pacts with slinky goddesses. I hurt before I even start moving. My ankle throbs in time with the bites on my thigh. Hazily the thought drifts through my head that it might be like that from now on. Rolling onto my back, I look out the window. The clouds above the city glow a dirty yellow, hanging low and heavy like the jaundiced belly of some beast. I wish I could see the stars, to see them like on that summer road trip when our car broke down on the two-lane highway in South Dakota and we slept in some farmer's pasture, stars like a million bottles smashed on the highway.

I stumble to the fridge. It's full, not just of orange juice, but fruits and vegetables and pre-cooked meats, like salami and sliced turkey. Preacher stocked it before the hit. I'll smile about that later. I pour myself a big glass of juice, then go to the small, battered writing desk I rescued from the alley by my building. It is paired with a thrift store office chair. From its one drawer, I withdraw my journal, bound in green cloth. I turn to a fresh page and fish a pen out of the drawer. I write last night's date at the top of the page and begin.

***

She washes my face, gently but thoroughly, then my neck. She traces my collarbone with her pinkie. I watch her face, which is utterly rapt, as if she is reading the secrets of the universe written in the braille of my body. She washes my breasts, hands moving in gentle circles. As her hands slide down towards my belly she leans in and flicks each nipple with a surprisingly rough tongue. I push them towards her, but she draws back. Her hands are under the water now. Her fingers play with the fringe of my hair. Now her hands glide over my pelvis and start a long, slow slide down my thigh, around my knee, along my calf, to my foot. Strong fingers find a knot in my arch and knead it briefly.

Then she bends my leg so my knee is up and out of the water, her gentle strength irresistible. Finally her mouth touches me. She kisses the inside of my knee. I shiver. Slowly, so slowly, she begins to brush her lips down the inside of my thigh. My hips lift. Her face is under the water now and I feel a slight prick as she gently slides her fangs under my skin. A slow, languorous wave of pleasure rolls outward from where her mouth is on me. A moan escapes my lips.

We stay like this for eternity. Wave after slow wave of exquisite sensation emanate from where she penetrates me. We are connected in one live circuit. I sense her huge hunger like a physical thing. My hands are in her hair, and I moan softly, over and over. Vaguely I wonder if she is feeding too slowly to get a lethal does of the toxin.

She lifts her head and tries to sit up, but falls weakly back into the tub.

"Don't stop," I beg.

"I, I feel strange," she says haltingly. "I think maybe I should ..."

I push her face back under the water, her mouth back to my thigh, holding her down with both hands. She latches on, obedient to the need. I push her fangs in deeper, deeper. I am enveloped in warmth and ecstasy, our hearts beating in unison, slowing, we sink together into the black...

The pacemaker jolts my heart into motion. I flop about in the water until I remember where I am. All the pleasure is gone, but her fangs are still in me. It hurts. I pull her head up by the hair, pulling her fangs free. I try to push her limp form out of the tub, but I am too weak. She is a real corpse now.

I put the pen down, and mark my new place in the journal with the ribbon. My hand trembles. I need to sleep some more, and then eat. Beyond that is the void that is always my future more than a few days hence. Today is a miracle.

14

Donna

Momma always said, "The most embarrassing people are the ones who pretend they are somethin' that they ain't. You get embarrassed for them just being around them." Donna tells her daughters that every time they tell her she ought to dress up and go out dancing like she used to do. Now she is getting embarrassed for herself, waiting in a big, fancy car with gangsters to kidnap some badass monster hunter, or some such. It's ridiculous, but the Covenant makes for strange times and desperate actions.

Her lower back is beginning to get stiff despite the deep, leather seats of the Cadillac. They've been sitting in the back of this car for almost an hour, waiting. She has to pee, and she keeps puffing on her inhaler because the mafia bitch smokes.

"We sure they're coming?"

"Theodore, explain it to the lady again. She has a bad memory."

Despite the insult, she grins inside. Hearing the Wall addressed as Theodore by his mother almost makes this worth it.

"That uptight cunt in the ..."

"Language, Theodore."

Donna can't hide her smile this time.

"Our informant in the Vampire Mayor's office knows she has the dentist appointment because of the insurance. One of our guys has had eyes on the place. She went in on time, hasn't come out. Must have some fucked up teeth."

"What do I tell you about cursing, Theodore?"

"Ah, Ma, it's how all the guys talk."

"What do I tell you?"

"It makes me sound dumb."

"It makes you sound common. You are not common, Theodore, you are going to run this town someday."

Donna looks out her window and tries not to chuckle. The idea that that dumb slab of meat could run a lemonade stand is ridiculous. His Momma, though, is a different story. For the hundredth time, Donna wonders if the city they get after they break the Covenant will be any better.

Someone catches her eye on the sidewalk. Hard to miss someone who moves like that while showing legs like those. It's Penny. For a couple of years, she has been going to the Night Fowl and has never seen Penny outside that place, like she doesn't exist outside those grimy walls. Now here she is.

"There she finally fucking is," the Wall grunts out. His mother leans forward and smacks the back of his head, with a hand festooned with large rings.

"Ow!"

Donna looks incredulously at the gangsters and back at the woman approaching on the sidewalk.

"Seriously? She's our vampire hunter?"

The mafia bitch leans across to look out the window.

"Don't be ridiculous. Obviously, she isn't the killer, but she isn't half bad bait. Pop the trunk, Theodore."

The Wall leans forward and Donna hears a click behind her. Is this really happening? Is she really participating in a kidnapping? Penny is almost even with the nose of the big car. The fake blond sociopath next to her elbows her in the ribs.

"You're up, Ms. Legit. Stall her for thirty seconds is all you gotta do."

"But I know her. She's just a waitress in a shitty bar. This has to be a mistake."

The Wall grunts from the front seat. "That's what I been tryin' to tell them."

The mafia bitch's eyes lose their shallow mirth and become all ice and calculation.

"She's the target. If she knows you, that makes it even easier."

Donna stares at the woman, wondering if she has lost her mind.

"Get out there and do your job, or it's going to be you in the trunk."

Donna takes a deep breath, opens the heavy car door and steps out onto the sidewalk, directly in Penny's path. The young woman stops and stares.

"Donna?"

"Hi, Penny. Weird seeing each other out of context, isn't it."

Penny looks Donna up and down in confusion, not noticing the Wall get out of the car behind her. He can be quiet for such a big man. The Wall's huge hand covers her mouth, while his other hand picks her easily up off the pavement. The mafia bitch has the trunk open, and it's over so fast Donna's head spins. The wall shakes his hand in pain.

"That dumb whore bit me!"

"Of course she did, what did you expect, a kiss? Now stop being a baby and get in the car," replies his mother.

Donna is still standing on the sidewalk blinking when the mafia bitch grabs her arm and pulls her into the car.

"Jesus, Mary and Joseph you two are useless. I might as well have come by myself," mutters the mafia bitch.

"Ma, how am I ever gonna have the confidence to lead if you are tearing me down all the time?"

"Shut up your psycho babble and drive. You get confidence by doing things, like kidnapping dangerous persons in broad daylight and getting away with it."

She looks at Donna and shakes her head.

"Kids, am I right?"

All this time the woman in the trunk has been kicking at the trunk lid so hard that Donna thinks something has to break, either Penny or the car. Now she switches to kicking the back of the seat. She is screaming.

"You assholes are so dead. You have no idea who will come for me. I'm valuable property, you motherfuckers. Let me go and maybe they won't cut you into too many pieces." Each sentence is punctuated by a solid kick to the back of the seat. The mafia bitch smiles.

"I like her."

15

TOM

T om squirms in the metal folding chair and fidgets with the lucky coin in his left pocket. He hates the smell of this Geezer Club, talcum powder and piss, but he has to admit that no one notices what happens in the Rec Room of an old folks home. Although you would think that some nurse would be curious about what was up at this time of night. He flips over the discarded bingo card on the folding table he is sitting at. On the back is written in looping cursive script, "Meet me behind the garden shed after dinner and I will blow your mind, among other things." He chuckles. A lot more goes on in these places than people think.

They lead Penny in, then, that genetic freak and his mother. She has some kind of cloth bag over her head, and her hands are behind her back. The Wall has three long, red scratches on his face. Barely missed losing an eye, it looks like. Tom isn't surprised. They take her to the focal point of the room, where the podium and projector screen are, and sit her in one of these torture device folding chairs. Mama Perelli says something to her boy, and he snatches the bag off Penny's head.

"Ow!" She turns around as far as she can and spits.

"Leave me some hair, you gorilla."

The Wall raises his hand but is stopped by the geezer behind the podium grabbing his elbow. Tom finds he is gripping the edge of the table with both hands. The geezer looks like he might have a coronary.

"Her? She's the assassin?" says the Geezer.

"Take a look at my face, Pops. She ain't no wilting flower."

Penny catches site of the old man and does a double take. "What the hell are you doing here?" she demands.

"This is my place. We are at the Home."

"Now why did I put a bag over her head if we're just going to tell her?" the Wall whines.

Momma Perelli looks from captive to geezer.

"Does everyone in the city know this cutie?"

Penny is still gawking at the old man. The geezer says, "Just from the neighborhood. Passing acquaintances."

There is an awkward silence, then Penny tosses back her head and laughs. She chokes out something that sounds like, "Good one." Tom frowned. He can't blame her for being hysterical, but it doesn't bode well.

"We should ... continue with the introductions," the Geezer stammers. You have met Momma Perelli, trusted lieutenant in a prominent Italian community organization. Her son, Theo. In the other corner over there are the twins, Michael and Ruth, from the vampire community."

Tom has never seen Penny shaken. In other circumstances, he might have enjoyed seeing her lose the attitude. He clinches his jaw, waiting his turn.

"At the middle table are Donna Clark and Greta Finch, from the human Mayor's office and Vampire Mayor's office, respectively."

Penny mutters something Tom cannot hear, eyes wide.

"And Tom Willard," the geezer pauses, "... a man who knows things."

That snaps her out of it. She tries to leap out of her chair, but the Wall grabs her by the hair.

"You son of a bitch! You got Francis killed. Maybe his whole family. You sold me out to be the Vampire Mayor's bitch. Fuck you. Fuck you before you were born and fuck you after you're dead!"

Tom unclenches his jaw. "You can't put Francis on me. He was already dead."

"Oh, well I guess you're OK with yourself then."

"Penny ..." the old man tries to interject.

"You can't trust him! Whatever fucked up little cabal you have here, he'll turn on you. He's a rat."

"Penny," the old man says in that kind but firm voice that Tom has studied, but is unable to emulate. "We know Tom ratted you out to the Vampire Mayor. Don't expect you to be OK with that, but there were extenuating circumstances. "

"Jesus, are you really defending him?" Penny asks.

"You can't blame him for protecting family," says Donna. "In a way, that's why we're all here."

Confusion mixes with rage on Penny's face.

"What family? He's the perfect bachelor. It's like he's a cartoon."

Tom had promised to let the others talk, but he can no longer keep his mouth shut. He jumps to his feet.

"It's like this. I rent a room from my brother and his wife. Nice little place in the suburbs. They have two kids, Johnny and Paula. I babysit, that's the main reason they let me stay there. Take some pressure off Mom and Dad, right? I'm Uncle Tommy, and any night I'm not hitting on you at the Night Fowl, I'm with those kids. Tomorrow I'm taking them to that science museum with all the hands-on stuff."

He stops to get his breath. He is revealing too much, but the words have tumbled out. Penny is staring at him, blank-faced.

"I couldn't risk those kids for you, Penny. I'm not going to apologize."

They are all looking at him. One of the creepy vampire twins speaks.

"What else did you tell them, while you were being gallant?"

"We have already covered that ground." More firmness in the old man's voice this time, less kindness. He does not like the vamps. "Tom had no reason to tell them about us. They wanted to know who killed the mobster Vampire, and we weren't involved. Remember, our source on the inside confirmed the Mayor does not suspect a conspiracy." He gestures at the Vamp Mayor's secretary. She nods and replies.

"At first he suspected something organized, but once he met Bad Penny, as he calls her, and observed her kill of Mistress Violet, he was satisfied that she is a simple predator."

Momma Perelli snorts but makes no further comment.

Penny says something too low to hear. Everyone returns their attention to her.

"Why didn't you warn her? Do they know she was your Mistress? Why didn't you warn her about me?"

"I did."

"You did? But ..."

"She believed she overmatched you enough that she could play with you, like a cat with a mouse. She was like that."

"Clearly she was also wrong," the old man says, still standing behind the podium looking for all the world like a proud Principal.

"Who are you people? I know some of you, but what is this?" She makes a gesture with her arm that takes in the whole room.

"We are a group of," the old man hesitates, "people who stand against the Covenant."

"We have a name," hisses one of the vampires in the corner. "She gave us a name," hisses the other twin. "We are the Perfidus," the first twin, "and she is our leader." "Was our leader, until you slew her, " second twin, "filthy snake-in-the-grass," they finish in unison.

"The Perfidus? Covenant? Is this some kind of twisted role playing game?"

Donna speaks. "Vampires are all about the melodrama, Honey."

"I do not think we need to explain vampires to her," says the vampire's secretary. She stares at Penny like Tom's nephew sometimes stares at bugs he has trapped under a jar. Tom keeps the creepy ass twins in the corner of his eye. Violet was their leader, and with her gone who knows what they will do. No doubt they could kill everyone in this room in under two minutes. Well, maybe not Penny. He feels another stab of guilt, like a needle in the eye.

"Oh for fuck's sake, just tell her straight out," he says to the room.

The old man nods. "You see, Penny, the three powers of the city, the human government," he points to the Donna, "the vampire government," he points to the Ice Queen, "and organized crime," he points to Momma Perelli, "have joined together in a pact they call the Covenant. They cooperate instead of fighting each other, each faction getting what they want, without having to worry about being interfered with by the others."

"If what you want ... is to be tamed ... and fed garbage ... for eternity." The creepy twins were in full finish each other's sentence mode.

Penny shakes her head. "Everyone knows the police don't investigate Vamp kills, at least everyone that admits Vamps exist. But that's just fear. And the mob's been buying favors since time began. It's still hard to believe humans work with vampires to the degree you are talking about."

Momma Perelli has taken a seat next to Donna. "This is a whole new level of cooperation and coordination. Trust me."

"Trust you? You mean because you kidnapped me to bring me to this Mad Hatter's party in an old folks home?"

Tom speaks up. "She has a point."

The creepy twins speak in creepy unison. "How can one so naive assist us?"

"She's mentally deficient. I told ya, she's just a great pair of legs," sneered the Wall.

"She is a weapon," says the Vampire Mayor's secretary, "to be aimed at a target and fired. No more, no less."

"We should kill her now," hisses Twin One.

Penny tries to jump out of the Wall's grip, but that's not going to work. Tom's stomach hurts. He is the lowest lowlife on this totem pole. He won't be able to do squat if they decide to hurt Penny.

"Whoa, the Wall don't waste the best piece of ass in town like that. She's mine now."

Momma Perelli jumps to her feet. "How many times have I told you not to refer to yourself in the third person? It's pathetic."

"She is a human being, and she deserves an explanation. Stop the bickering."

It's all steel in the old man's voice, now. Steel forged storming some beach in Europe or the South Pacific, Tom can't remember which. He had been the only one who could ever check Dark Violet.

He chewed his nails while they laid it out for her. It's a habit he kicked long ago. Can't have a killer handshake with ragged nails. Amateurs thought it was just about firmness, but people do not buy expensive cars from a guy with working class hands.

The various conspirators take turns explaining how the factions don't just leave each other alone, they are trying to mesh into an integrated system. The city funnels victims to the vampires through institutions like old folks' homes, prisons and shelters of various kinds. The Mob gets lucrative contracts to operate those places. The vampires restrict their diet to the unfortunates funneled to them. The Mob backs off some of their traditional crime. Both the criminals and the vampires pay taxes through their legitimate business holdings. Law enforcement leaves everyone alone and concentrates on living to collect their pensions. It's a far cry from the long running, multi-party guerrilla war that was going on before the current Vampire Mayor took office and started building alliances, laying the groundwork for today's Covenant. You have to admire it, from a certain perspective.

"It is an impressive accomplishment, mostly down to the Vampire Mayor," says the geezer to sum up.

No one speaks for a while after that, giving Penny a chance to take it all in.

"So, you guys are what, the malcontents who want to return to the bad old days of street war where civilians like me get caught in the crossfire?"

Oh, shit. He never thought that Penny might think the Covenant was a good thing. The Vampire Mayor's secretary laughs, something he has never heard before. It is a surprisingly deep, throaty sound to come out of that bureaucratic bot.

"Oh, my, comfortable in the system already? Addicted to a paycheck so soon? Even the Vampire Mayor thought you a rebel of potentially legendary status. How droll."

"I hate working for that monster," Penny shoots back. She shivers. "But joining your little revolutionary book club sounds like the surest way to get dead I've heard of in a long time."

The geezer frowns at Penny.

"Penny, there are more innocent casualties now than ever. The entire city is becoming a more and more efficient slaughterhouse. The evilness of it is staggering."

"Yeah, show me someone who's innocent. What do you want from me?"

"We want you to help us end it."

"Right, be your good little foot soldier, take orders from you instead of the Vamp Mayor. Die sooner but more righteous, that about right?"

"We ... suspect that you ... are part of ... its genesis."

Penny looks at the vampires in confusion.

"Huh?"

"The Vampire ... Mayor was struggling ... to get compliance from ... his constituents. His plan ... is counter to ... basic vampire ... nature. But then a ... man slew his ... mistress and took ... her menagerie. It is ... believed he had ... help from someone ... in the ... menagerie. A ripple ... of fear swept ... through the vampire ... community. They ceded their ... independence to ... the Mayor's ... plan. You are ... known to be ... an associate of ... this man. Where did you ... get your ... first taste of ... killing, Bad Penny?"

Penny sits very still and very quietly.

"You really have no choice, chickadee," Momma Perelli speaks up. "Now that you know about us, you either join us or we kill you."

A pained look crosses the geezer's face, but he doesn't contradict the mobster.

"What do I have to do?"

"Kill the Vampire Mayor."

Penny's eyes get wide.

"So you're recruiting for suicide missions. No fucking way. I will not be your cannon fodder."

"Penny, we know you kill vampires," the old man says. Dark Violet was the next most dangerous vampire, after the Vampire Mayor. You won't be alone. You will be part of a larger operation."

She sneers at the old man. "Oh yeah, there going to be an extraction team ready to pull me out in a hail of bullets if things go south? Maybe an elite squad of octogenarians led by you and your friends from the bench?"

What is that about? There are no benches in the Rec Room, just the damn folding chairs.

"Not like that, no." The geezer shakes his head.

"What good is it going to do you? There will just be a new Vamp Mayor, and you will still have to deal with the other factions."

"The Vampire Mayor forged the Covenant. He is the linchpin. Removing him is the best chance we have."

"What chance do you half-a-dozen ..." she looks around the room ... "things have, even with the head vamp gone?"

"Oh, it's not just us, chickadee. Plenty of the Family are sick to our stomachs of betraying our species to the Fangs." She points to the twins. "

"You and your muscle take him out, then."

Momma Perelli looks at Donna.

"We got our own part to play, Honey."

"What does that mean?"

"As you pointed out, the Vampires are only one faction of the Covenant. We must cut off all three heads of the beast that preys on our city.

"It must happen at the same time," adds the Vamp Mayor's secretary. "Otherwise we are too vulnerable to reprisals from the other factions."

The geezer nods. "It was decided that the Family would remove the human Mayor, city forces would eliminate the head of the Family ..."

"... and our ... mistress would slaughter ...the vampire tyrant ... and bath ... in his ... blood."

I can't help picturing Dark Violet covered in blood from so many slaughtered people, Francis' blood. I bend over in my chair, holding my stomach, trying not to puke on my expensive, leather shoes.

"You can see the current deficiency in our plan," I hear the Vamp Mayor's secretary say.

"We need you, Penny. The whole city needs you, every friend, child, parent, lover, everyone."

"You killed ... the Mistress .. you .. Must fulfill ... her mission."

It is quiet for a moment, everyone catching their breath.

"If I say no."

"Sorry, chickadee. This isn't one of those choice situations."

She looks at the old man, who is looking a little more slumped, a little more gray.

"Are you what passes for a leader here? You just going to let them kill me if I say no to this suicide mission?"

The geezer looks down for a moment. There's no way the old man could stop the vamps and the gangsters from killing her to shut her up. He looks back up and meets Penny's eyes.

"Sorry it has to be this way, Ma'am. War is Hell."

16

BAD PENNY

The gangster bitch waves cheerfully at me as the big, black car pulls into traffic. I have a little sympathy for the Wall now, just a little. They did not drop me off on my street, too conspicuous. They also did not drop me off on the same street they kidnapped me from, which was a shame because I had been on my way to my favorite lunch spot as a little treat to myself, and seeing as how I will be leaving the city for good tonight, I will not ever taste Juanita's carnitas breakfast scramble again. Yes, my favorite lunch is breakfast. What can I say, I'm an iconoclast.

I don't know how long I'll survive in another city. There will be vamps. Vamps are everywhere, like cockroaches. How long will I be able to satisfy the Need and live? Here survival has been because of my arrangement with the Good Doctor, but recent events made it clear that arrangement is temporary. Between the Vampire Mayor and the Perfidus, I won't last a month here. Plus Preacher would get himself killed trying to protect me or avenge me. I have to get out of this city tonight.

A big, silver car pulls to the curb a little ahead of me and both passenger doors swing open. The Vampire Mayor's own Effie Perine steps quickly out.

"Oh for fuck's sake, haven't ..."

She gives a quick, sharp shake, "No," of her head, as some muscle I have never seen gets out of the driver's side.

"The Vampire Mayor requests an appointment, Miss Penny, immediately."

I stop in my tracks. "Seriously?"

Before I know it, she has me in the backseat. I am crammed in between her and another goon. Apparently, I require a lot of handling. Both of us are wearing skirts, and my right thigh is pressed against her left. Anywhere our skin touches she feels like she is running a fever of a hundred and ten. Her face is a little flushed like maybe she is excited by getting some action outside the office. The little smile on her face is as mocking as ever, and her eyes are frozen marbles. When she puts her hand on my knee, I'm sure she can feel me shiver.

"It seems we are going to get to know each other well, Bad Penny."

She leaves her hand there as we crawl through traffic, but she looks out the window as if disinterested in her company in the car. This allows me to look down her shirt with the illusion she isn't aware. Trying not to panic about seeing the Vampire Mayor, I distract myself by visualizing taking her hand and guiding it under my skirt. I have all but forgotten the goons until the one in the back seat with us speaks.

"Hey, Charlie, what do you say we have a little fun with these two hotties after the Mayor is done with them?"

"No can do. Strict orders from the boss, its hands off with these two."

The one next to me grunts.

"Always the same, the high and mighty keep the best for themselves."

"You said it, brother." I surprise him by replying. "That's why when you see what you want, you have to take it. It's the only way you're going to get it."

He stares at me. She chuckles and moves her hand a little further up my leg. I'm debating sticking my tongue in her ear when the car turns down an alley. Shit, that probably means we are there. She takes her hand off my leg and looks at me, no smile this time.

"When I let you out, there will be a door. We are to send you in on your own and wait for you. We will take you home after your appointment is over."

A wave of relief almost makes me dizzy. She is expecting me to come back out. The car stops. She gets out and extends a hand to help me. Once I am out she straightens my collar, then brushes my hair away from my forehead. I swear to god she is going to kiss me. I start to lean in and she steps back.

"Remember, you obey and you survive."

"Like I can resist obeying him."

That mocking smile returns to her face briefly.

"Oh, but that is why you are here, Bad Penny."

Shit. Shit. Shit.

She nods at an unmarked steel door in the brick wall of the alley and gets back in the car. I hope she is going to be OK after I egged on the goons like I did. Then I square my shoulders and open the door.

Pitch black inside, of course. The squeal of the door hinges echoes in a vast open space. As soon as the door is open, my First Bite begins to itch like mad, as if the thick, steel door was some kind of insulation for vampire essence. I put one foot on the threshold and push against the pull that is like a wire stretching from my chest into the dark.

"Come in, Penny." Hammers on sheet metal, I am pulled instantly into the dark. "Shut the door."

I'm not aware of obeying, but now I'm stumbling forward in the black, blind, reckless, almost running.

"Stop."

I skid to a stop, vaguely aware of my ankle's protests. I am panting like I just ran around the block.

"I want your mind clear enough to understand, Penny, and I fear my proximity hinders your thinking. I should have considered that at our first meeting. It's my own fault, maybe, that you did not carry out my instructions."

"I followed your instructions. I killed Dark Violet for you."

"Where is my proof?" Hammers beating double time on sheet metal. "The finger you sent with her gaudy signet ring? I told you to bring the body to me. Where is it?"

My legs stop trembling and my tongue uncleaves from the roof of my mouth. I am going to die now.

"I had another use for the body. That finger is proof enough; you know damn well she's gone, that there is a hole in the city where she used to be. I did the job, you aren't getting the body, deal with it."

There is silence for half a dozen slow, resignedly calm heartbeats, then a low chuckle.

"You are a piece of work, my bad, Bad Penny. Because you amuse me, I'm giving you one more chance than I should. You have to understand the consequences if you defy me again, however."

A spotlight blazes into life, momentarily blinding me. When I can see again, I stare in shock. The light illuminates a photograph that has been blown up to life size. It is a picture of a nondescript man walking down a tree-lined street that is definitely not in the city.

"Your brother, Steven. You haven't seen him in years, but still, he is blood.."

Another light pops on. This time it is an older woman, about sixty, waiting at what is obviously the Argyle stop.

"Your Aunt Simone. Her you see at least once a month. By all appearances, she is fond of you."

I try to speak, to ask how, but I am mute. More lights pop on, revealing photos of Penny's Irregulars, and finally, a picture of Preacher behind the counter at the soup kitchen, filling a bowl and looking as human and vulnerable as I have ever seen him.

"If you defy me again, Penny, you will next see them in my collection."

What seems like a thousand lights come to life above my head. They reveal a constellation of coffin-sized transparent boxes, suspended from the ceiling at varied heights, moving up and down in a silent circle through the air like a giant mobile. Each box is somehow illuminated from within, and each contains a body, suspended in clear fluid. It is grisly and beautiful and I think I am going to vomit. Suddenly the lights in all the boxes but one one go out. It sails slowly and gently through the darkness and contains two bodies instead of one. One of the corpses is Frances, the other is a woman I might recognize from a folded and faded photo taken from a wallet.

I don't know how long I've been screaming when he slaps me, sending me staggering and then falling on my ass. He looms over me, back-lit by the ghostly light of the flying coffin.

"Now you understand, Bad Penny, that you are mine. Do better next time."

The light above goes out, and he is gone. I am sobbing in the blackness when the hinges of the steel door squeal and a less dark rectangle appears in the distance.

"Come here, Penny. It is time to go home."

There is only one goon in the car now, the driver, so there is room for me to lie down in the back seat and rest my head in her lap. She silently strokes my hair until they drop me a block from my apartment. It's bad, that short walk home. Memories surface, like bloated bodies. Memories of chains and cages, of cold, dark days and nights without division. Monotony so extreme that it was almost that that drove me over the edge. All the while craving the bite of the Mistress vampire that held me there. Only Preacher saved me. No. It was my hand that struck down the Master. My hand that freed us. This very hand that is trembling as I try to get the key into the lock on my door. Finally, I stumble in.

There is a cake on my table. It is frosted in blue, with balloons done in primary colors, and these words in green icing, "On Completion of Your First Assignment." I reach out and gouge a divot in the icing with my finger. It is real. I have just put my finger in my mouth, and the grainy icing brings weird, incongruous memories of birthdays, when I notice something wrong with my table. It's the same old chipped Formica, but it is too tall. Frowning, I sit in one of my red vinyl chairs. The broken spring does not jab me in the butt. I shift around on it, but there are no lumps. It looks like my chair, but it isn't.

I look up at the picture hanging next to the front door. It is the same print of Caravaggio's Blah Blah, but it is in a different frame, darker wood with rounded corners. I look at my bed. The wool bedspread has a similar pattern but with more greens and blues, less red. Twisting around, I see that my clock is still analog, with Roman numerals, but the hands are bronze instead of black. The jade plant sitting on the counter is in the same pot, I think, but looks larger and healthier. Feeling shaky again, I go to my closet. It is full of clothes that look like clothes I would wear, but I bought none of them.

Some tea. Some ginger tea will settle my stomach. When I get my mug from the dish dryer, it is not the Florida SeaWorld mug my little brother gave me. It is a California SeaWorld mug. Nothing here is mine, it's all his. I am his.

17

DONNA

When Donna's Momma was older, she spent a lot of time at the corner bar. Donna does not remember her drinking hardly at all until she was almost sixty. Once the kids and grandkids were all out of the house, the loneliness and all those piled up disappointments of a lifetime ate at her. She started telling Donna things like, "Find yourself a good bar and keep it in your back pocket like a rainy day fund, 'cuz you're gonna need it someday." She also told Donna, "Pick a bar like you pick a lover. If you like your lovin' with crisp, folded napkins and shiny, polished wood, pick a bar like that. But if you like it a little sloppy and stinky, then that is the kind of bar you want, too." Donna can just imagine what Momma would say if she walked in here and found her daughter at her regular table at the Night Fowl.

"Lord, Girl, I hope your pussy isn't as sticky as this floor." Grey haired Momma would have said that. Younger Momma would have just grabbed Donna by the wrist and dragged her out of there, and been rigidly silent all the way home. Truth is, Momma wasn't right about everything. Donna doesn't blame her. No one is. Donna's bar, with its sticky floor and patina of despair, is nothing like her love life. Momma sure was wrong about that safe government job, too.

Three nights she has been at her table, eating greasy nachos and ordering watery beer from that cow Angela, waiting for Penny to show. She finally did, tonight. Bad Penny, funny how quickly that stuck once the Vamp Mayor christened her. She has been avoiding Donna, but she'll have to check on her, eventually.

Donna scans the bar again, trying to imagine which of these sorry specimens is a plant, a low down dirty traitor to their species. Hard to believe the Vamp Mayor isn't keeping track of such a valuable asset. Tom is sitting with his back to her. She likes to keep one eye on him. Real canary in the coal mine, that one. Real strong survival instincts.

Last night, Wednesday, was their card night. It was her turn to pick, so she brought the deck, they played Gin and she won. Next week will be his turn, they'll play poker, and he will win. If they are alive next week. Odds are one of them won't be. That would be a shame. The other card night tradition is they go to the winner's place after. He's a dog, but he smells nice, and he has soft hands.

That's how it started, with the two of them all limp and sweaty and tangled up in the sheets, hesitantly talking about what they saw, what they knew, knew that their families weren't safe in this town, knew that the Covenant had to be broken. They weren't anyone special, but they had contacts. Slowly they reached out, testing the waters, bringing together the enemies of their enemies. Sure, the mobsters and the vampires and the war heroes ended up leading, but make no mistake, they were the genesis, these two nobodies keeping each other company on card night.

Because she is getting all maudlin, she doesn't notice Penny's approach until Penny pulls out a chair next to her, spins it around and sits, straddling it like it's a sugar daddy who has been inattentive lately, giving her a crotch shot if she wanted it. Girls are not her flavor, but that girl could've done a better job of tempting Jesus in the desert than the Devil himself. It's a sad thing that Donna can not see any way Penny survives this.

"You know what I love about this place, is it is the only place I have ever been where truly anyone is welcome. Color, class, creed, it doesn't matter, because folks figure if you frequent this dump, you got your reasons. We're sitting in the lowest common denominator made concrete." She taps her foot loudly on the rough cement floor.

Penny's mouth twists into a bitter smirk, but her eyes are sad.

"You know what's weird, sometimes you see someone from in here, out there." Penny nods towards the door.

"I know, Girl, it was a trip seeing you at that party a few weeks ago. Speaking of, are you ready for tomorrow night?" asks Donna.

Penny freezes and turns a little paler than usual. "Tomorrow?"

"We've been waiting until we could talk to you before we scheduled that girls' night out we were discussing. Best to plan only one night ahead so nothing comes up that would interfere. You can be ready, right?"

No smirk now. Penny looks kind of like Momma when the doctor told her about the cancer.

"Sure, tomorrow, why not?"

"Remember, girls' night out, so don't go bringing along any of those menfolk who follow you around. That would ruin the vibe."

Penny knows who Donna means. She nods.

"Great." Donna slaps the table in front of her with both hands. "See you at eleven, then."

Penny nods again, this time the sadness in her eyes reaches her mouth. "Eleven." She stands. "Better not neglect the rest of the Irregulars."

"Better not."

18

BAD PENNY

You might think that taxi drivers would know not to take fares for the Vampire Quarter at night, and it used to be true, but apparently the Vampire Mayor likes visitors because the driver just leers at me and takes my money. Possibly the last vivid memory of my life is going to be the smell of whatever he ate for dinner, something with a lot of garlic. My phone vibrates. It is a text from Preacher.

"Hunting tonight?"

"Scouting," I reply, then turn off my phone. I'm not ghosting him because Donna told me to, but she is right. He would ruin everything trying to protect me, and probably get himself killed. He thinks he owes me forever, for freeing him from our vampire mistress, and because he chose me for her menagerie so he could have me. Truth is, he doesn't owe me a thing, and I sure as hell do not want him dying for me.

We are getting close. My Doctor's bag is on the seat next to me. I reach into it and pull out the stainless steel tube, remove the rubber stopper and swallow the contents, the familiar metallic tang filling my mouth. The driver checks me in the mirror.

"Getting ready for some fun! Real party girl, huh?"

"You have no idea."

I put the vial back in the bag, next to the still chilled bag of blood. The backup syringe is taped to the inside of my left arm. The cab squeals to a halt in front of Vampire Hall. I start to open my little purse, but the driver hops out, circles the car and opens the door for me.

"No charge for this destination. Complimentary service." He leers at me again. I consider kicking him in the balls, but I am on a mission, so I just give him my best go-fuck-yourself smile and get out of the cab, Doctor's bag in hand. He tips his stupid hat at me and is gone in a hurry.

This time I know the way, so I have no excuse for how long it takes me to reach the door up on the catwalk. My heart rate increases along with the burning of my First Bite. He is here, all right. I do not try to fight the effect of his presence. My vulnerability is my bait and my camouflage. Finally, I am standing in front of the door. I rap on the dense wood smartly twice and enter.

The secretary is behind her desk, exactly as she was on my previous visit. The only difference is she gives me a slight nod of recognition.

"Hello, Miss Penny."

"I called last night. I have an appointment."

"Yes, it is on the calendar. Please take a seat."

When I sit, I slide my Doctor's bag next to the club chair. She pretends not to notice, but my life likely depends on her bringing it to me after the Mayor has drained me. I can't relax in the sumptuous leather chair. Perching on the edge of the seat, I put one hand under my skirt and massage my inner thigh, long past caring what she might think, watching me. To my surprise, she gets up from her chair, comes out from behind her desk, and crosses the narrow room to sit in the chair next to me. My heart takes a major jolt in my chest when she puts her hand up my skirt and rests it on top of mine. I meet her eyes.

"It is time."

She leans in and plants the most gentle, butterfly of a kiss on my lips, then stands, helping me to my feet, and gently propels me to the door of the Mayor's office. I look back over my shoulder at her at the last moment, then open the door and step in. I make it one step across the threshold before I freeze. Instead of the burly, bearded vampire behind the desk, there is a slim, severe blond woman in a lab coat.

"Doctor?"

Everything goes black.

19

DONNA

The big, black car glides silently through the darkness. No sounds or smells from the outside penetrate the hermetically sealed box of luxury on wheels. They have only what they bring with them, The Wall's shitty cologne, his Momma's chainsaw voice, and Donna's funk at the end of a long day of work and hopefully hidden fear.

"Will I die tonight? Will my city? This city that, shitty as it is, is my home?"

She expected the Wall to be nervously loud and profane, but he is tensely quiet, gripping the steering wheel until his hands turn white. The Mafia Bitch, on the other hand, is excitedly chatty, like they are on their way to a party, not to slaughter a man in his home. She goes over and over the plan.

"OK, Donna, your part again."

"Early today I called my contact at the PD, our liaison to the cops who are fed up with letting vampires and mobsters get off Scot free. She put out the word that tonight is the night they take out your boss."

"Former boss," Perelli interjects.

"Former boss. She also arranged to have the patrolman that was on guard duty at the Mayor's house go home sick."

"After he started his shift, so there wouldn't be time to find a replacement," Perelli interjects again.

"Yes. Finally, about thirty minutes ago, I called the Mayor at home, from a burner phone so it can't be traced after. I told him the application for funds from the Feds had to be mailed by midnight and he still needed to sign it. He said he would come to City Hall, but I offered to bring it to his house, instead."

The Mafia bitch picks up where Donna left off.

"I am about your height and build. You loaned me one of your hideous pantsuits. In the dark, he won't be able to tell it's not you until it is too late. I double tap him in the chest, pop pop and your little trouble at City Hall is taken care of."

Donna continues. "Our cops visit your boss and take care of your problem."

"And just like that, I'm Queen of Crime."

Perelli's smile is full of gold.

"You guys really think Penny can take out the Vamp Mayor," comes from the front, tense and low. Perelli puts both hands up in the air and waggles her fingers.

"Not a chance. That little number is finished. But with the cops and the crime families against him, we can handle him," answers his Momma.

No answer from the front. Donna doesn't think he likes that about Penny. You could almost count him an Irregular, and they are all a little in love with her. Or maybe he's just worried that the Vamp Mayor will come for his Momma. Hard to tell with primitives like him. They act human at the weirdest times.

They pull up to the gate of the community the Mayor lives in, and Donna tells the access code to the Wall. Despite the blasting AC, her pits are damp. She looks quickly around in all directions, looking for cop cars. Any around here tonight will not be friendlies. She hasn't seen any for the past ten blocks, and police presence inside the gated neighborhood is minimal. So far, so good.

They wind deep into the enclave to get to the Mayor's prime lot. Donna thought she would have to give the Wall constant instructions, but it seems he's memorized the route. His Momma is humming, and bouncing her knee in time with the thrumming of the engine.

"There it is," Perrelli points unnecessarily at the mini-mansion at the end of the cul-de-sac. She pulls her gun out of her waistband and checks whatever it is that people check when they are about to use one. The Wall parks the car one house over. They don't want Anthony to see the Mafia Bitch get out of this car or he'll know it isn't Donna.

"Here we go, kids. Keep your eyes open and try not to ruin your underwear. Momma's going to work."

She and the Wall get out of the car. He stays by the front of the car, ready as backup. She strolls up the sidewalk like the expected visitor she is. The first gunshots come when she has just started up the crushed gravel path to the front door. The sound makes Donna jump before she even knows what it is. When Momma Perrelli staggers to the side and drops to her hands and knees, Donna's brain catches up.

"Fuck."

The sound that comes out of the Wall is like something you might hear in the jungle, a scream of rage half strangled by despair. He has his gun out and is firing in the general direction of the house, but Donna isn't sure at what specifically until she sees the muzzle flashes in the dark.

Donna sits in the back seat of the car, stunned. This is not the way it was supposed to go. The sound of the gunshots is deafening, and she finds herself crouching down behind the seat, even though she knows the car is armored. She doesn't have a gun because she doesn't know how to even fire one. Then, for an instant, Momma is there in the car with her, not in her head, but a presence next to her. She shouts above the noise.

"Don't let fear of dyin' make you a coward. Life's mostly a shit-hole anyway, what you got to lose?"

Fuck it. She grabs the handle and pushes the heavy door open, kneeling down behind it. The Wall is also kneeling, using the front corner of the car as a shield while he reloads his gun. The Mafia Bitch is trying to belly crawl towards the car. The Wall finishes reloading and sees Donna crouching there. She makes eye contact, nods once, and then jumps out from behind the door and sprints towards his Momma. Gunshots ring out from behind her as the Wall starts shooting again. Perelli has almost reached the sidewalk, about twenty feet from the car. It takes an eternity to cross that space, expecting to be hit any moment, but she makes it.

Donna tries to help Perelli to her feet, but it's no use, she is barely conscious. Grabbing both wrists, Donna drags her down the sidewalk, leaving a trail of dark blood. Donna's left shoulder jerks, like it's been hit by a hammer. She can only pull with one arm now, they are not going to make it. Then a mountain of white charges up to them and scoops up the prone woman. The Wall turns his back on the muzzles flashing in the dark and pushes Donna ahead of him. When they get to the car Donna jumps in the still open door to the back and crawls to the far side. The Wall tosses his Momma in after her and turns. His back is a mosaic of crimson blooms. He must have taken several hits on the way to the car, shielding them with his huge body. As Donna stares at the macabre but beautiful pattern, his head explodes. She screams as his body collapses. Bullets ping off the car. The windshield is a spider web, but she can see figures running towards them. She clambers over the seat and throws the still running engine into gear. They roar into the night, careening across the road because she can only steer with one arm, and damn is the other one starting to hurt.

20

BAD PENNY

It's the burning strain on my shoulders that drags me back into consciousness, that and the pain of metal digging into my wrists. I know I'm hanging by my arms before I open my eyes. I can just barely stand on the tip of my toes, taking some of the pressure off my shoulders. When I open my eyes, I am blinded by a bright light and close them again. A cold, familiar voice comes from my right.

"I'm not used to my specimens waking up."

I turn towards the sound and spit. A soft gasp tells me I hit my mark. I struggle to open my eyes against the bright light, and squint at the nearby silhouette.

"How long have you worked for the Vampire Mayor?"

"Approximately three years, two years before I found you." Still wiping the side of her face with her hand.

"Why?"

"Money. All researchers are looking for funding, always."

"But why would he fund research for Vampire poison?"

"Don't be naive. Who would have more need of a weapon against vampires than the one who wants to rule them?"

I shift my weight on my toes, trying to relieve more of the strain on my shoulders. I look up. There are manacles around my wrists, connected to chains that stretch up into the darkness. I am in a large, industrial space, almost surely the Vampire Mayor's warehouse. I look down at myself.

"Naked? Really?"

"We had to make sure you did not have any more of these hidden," says a voice from just outside the pool of light that spotlights me. The Vampire Mayor's secretary steps forward, holding up the syringe that had been taped to my arm. "Plus," she walks up close and reaches out her other hand, running a finger between my breasts, down my belly, around my mound and stopping on my first bite scar, "it is fun to watch you squirm."

"Why you? Why betray us? It was him that made me kill Violet."

The beautiful, frozen mask of a face contorts into an ugly picture of rage.

"I gave myself to her completely, body and soul, and she gave me to him, to be her spy. I was nothing but a tool. She betrayed me, not the other way around."

"But I'm the one who killed her. If you hated her that much ..."

She slaps me across the face so hard I almost black out again. She steps close and whispers in my ear.

"I will never forgive you for snuffing out that magnificent dark flame, no matter how much I hated her. I warned her, in the end, but she was so sure you were no danger to the Great Dark Violet. Now the flame in the dark is snuffed out forever."

Her expression melts from anger into despair. She leans her forehead against mine.

"It is not your fault. You were just doing what is in your nature, same as her, same as all of us. Perhaps I would have spared you if I could."

Suddenly there's a stinging pain in my armpit. "Ah, Jesus!"

The Good Doctor has a syringe in me. Normally sandwiched between two pushy blonds would be alright, but this is ridiculous.

"What are you doing?"

"Getting a blood sample."

"I thought you knew everything about your lab rat?"

"She's making sure you are free of that nasty poison, so I can eat you."

Hammers on sheet metal. The secretary steps away, staying just within the circle of light. He steps into the light. My traitorous thigh begins to burn.

"I'm going to keep you a long time. You are going to be the aperitif I sip before retiring for the day." He gestures at the Secretary. "I've promised Ms. Finch she can play with you in my off hours."

The Good Doctor speaks up. "I found her in the first place. I should have priority."

The glare she gets for that would have made me turn and run, but she holds her ground.

"Ah, yes, those macabre experiments you want to try. You can have her when we're tired of her. Now run along and do those tests. I'm impatient to finally taste this one."

She extracts the needle from my body and stalks out of my line of site. I shout over my shoulder. "Cheer up, Doc, maybe they'll even give me to you alive."

With my head turned, I feel his approach, rather than see it. There is a pressure pushing against me, as if his presence extends beyond his physical body. My first bite flares, eclipsing the sensations of my strained shoulders and calves. He stops an arm's length away, his eyes roaming every inch of my stretched out naked body. I can sense his hunger urging him closer, yet he restrains himself. I moan. He chuckles.

"I was right about you. You want it more than I do. Your self-absorption is so great you haven't even thought about what we're doing to your friends, have you?

His last sentence is like a bucket of cold water.

"Had you forgotten this isn't all about you? About the elaborate plan to cut off the three heads of the Covenant? About your conspirators trying to undo all my work and drag us back into the past?"

Oh, god, the others.

"Thanks to Ms. Finch, we know about all of it. We have the element of surprise, and we will kill them all, tonight. Including your precious preacher man."

My heart lurches in my chest. "He doesn't even know about it. He's not part of this."

"He's been a thorn in my side ever since he and you destroyed Maria and took her menagerie. I cannot let that stand. It's becoming mythic among the vampires."

"Didn't your attempts to take him out before backfire? You'll be wasting vampires."

"Then I will send them again, and again, and again until he is destroyed."

I feel despair start to wash over me, the despair Preacher has helped me fight off time and again, my beautiful Preacher.

"Now there's the truth dawning on you. It's almost a shame to break you, Bad Penny. Almost. Now the fun here is over for a while. I'll be back when we know you are safe to eat.

21

— • —

TOM

No one was surprised when Tom offered to close tonight. The boss gave him a knowing smile, expecting him to make some good off-book cash for her. The suburbs are a shitty place to hide, with their tidy yards and wide roads. No, he would have a better chance here at the dealership, than at his room at the house, a better chance if something goes wrong, and something always goes wrong.

Tom has a cot here, because of his frequent nocturnal clients. Usually, he watches game show reruns on the TV in the lobby while snacking from the vending machine, to which he has a key, but tonight he wants to be alert. Finished the crossword hours ago, and he only has a couple of sudoku left in his book. It's going to be a long night.

At least he didn't have to have crappy takeout for dinner. His sister-in-law, Beverly, had leftovers and packed him up some pot roast. She's a real peach, always cheerful, a good cook, the first person to lend a hand. Tom told his brother she was too good for him, that he was smart to go for a good heart instead of looks. Philip said any woman is beautiful when she has your cock in her mouth. Got it figured out, his big brother. Always was smarter than Tom, or wiser, anyway.

He was the one who told Tom he should make a move on Donna. Came to the Night Fowl a couple of times for beers and liked her right away. Tom only had eyes for Penny, but Philip slapped him upside the head, told him she was trouble. He was right, of course.

Philip wasn't thrilled when Tom woke him up in the middle of the night and told him he had to get the family out of town. Asked Tom if he was on shrooms again, said Tom must have finally lost it, babbling about conspiracies between Vamps and gangsters. Bev just rolled out of bed and started packing. Told Philip he should listen to his little brother once in a while, that Tom had a different kind of smarts. In the morning, right before they rolled out of town, she handed Tom the dinner she packed for him and kissed him on the cheek. Tom thinks there were tears in her eyes. She told him thanks for all the help with the kids, and good luck, and whispered that she'd put extra garlic in the roast. Philip just slammed the door on the way out. Tom can't blame him. As far as he sees it, Tom is either nuts or put his family in danger. Hard for him to understand that Tom did it to make them safer, so Jessie and Frank could grow up in a less evil city.

It's midnight, the hour of deeds done in the dark. Tom tried to talk Donna out of going, but she said it was her responsibility. She couldn't set someone up to be murdered and then just walk away, no matter how much they deserved it. She is supposed to text him when it's done, something cryptic that can't be used as evidence, later. He's got his phone on vibrate and alarm and is staring at it so hard he doesn't notice the SUV pull up right away.

It isn't until one of the dumb gorillas slams their car door that Tom looks up. That is just in time to see them point AK-47's at him through the glass front of the showroom. He ducks behind the counter to the sound of automatic gunfire and breaking glass. Shit. Shit. Shit. He crawls out from behind the courtesy counter and around the corner into the hall that leads back to the sales offices. Once around the corner he is up and running. The gunfire stops and they will be coming in to see if they got him.

Tom slams through the Employees Only door at the end of the hall and runs past the offices. Right before the bathrooms, he slides around the corner into a smaller hallway and stops in front of a door marked, Maintenance. Fumbling with his key ring, he hears shouts from the front. He finds the key and gets the door open. Once in, he locks the door behind him and turns on the little LED flashlight on his key chain. There is a hulking old furnace in the corner the size of a truck. Not used anymore, but too much trouble to remove. You wouldn't think there was much room behind it, and he thinks everyone but him has forgotten about the floor hatch between it and the wall. He pulls back the nasty old rug he had covered it with, opens the hatch and climbs partway down the ladder. Closing the hatch as quietly as he can, he tries to yank the rug back over it, but it's iffy if he managed to get it in place before he had to pull his hand in.

At the bottom of the ladder is an open cardboard box. Tom grabs the headlamp out of it and straps it to his head. Thank Jesus the batteries are still good. The light reveals another door in the opposite wall, a heavy, iron, seriously old looking door. Back in the day, this room would have been filled with coal. See, they had these tunnels under the city to deliver coal to the coal cellars. The tunnels aren't used anymore, but they are still there, with their boarded up and forgotten doors into basements all over town. When Tom found this entrance, he knew it was gold. Always good to have a back way out in case something goes wrong, and something always goes wrong.

One more thing to do before heading into the tunnels. The light from the headlamp plays over another pile of stuff in the corner. It looks like some kind of backpack with a hose and nozzle attached to it. Getting the flame thrower was easier than you might think if you know the right people. Nasty, dark places, tunnels. Never know what you're going to run into. Tom struggles to get the straps of the heavy contraption over his shoulders, slips through the groaning old door and shuts it behind him.

The headlamp is plenty bright in here, so when he rounds the first bend in the tunnel, he sees the two vamps right away, one leaning against the side, one clinging to the ceiling.

"Ah, and here he is, Charlie, just as the Mayor said he would be."

"Yeah, he figured a rat like this one would have naturally found the tunnels. That's why he's mayor, smart like that."

"Looks like he's got a toy, Charlie. What do you think that silly thing is that he's pointing at us?"

Tom pulls the trigger and the world catches on fire.

22

GEEZER

The light from the street light is not bright enough to read his watch, but it has glow-in-the-dark hands, 0100. Bill's bony old ass is not happy about sitting on this bench for an hour. He shifts again, trying to find a spot that doesn't hurt. One way or another, it's over now. There are more sirens than usual, and the flickering glare on the clouds of a fire somewhere in the city. Soon they'll send a messenger round to give him status, or no one will come, and that will be a message, also.

The door to the Home creaks open. Bill stiffens. It's common for the other inhabitants to be awake at night, but who the hell is coming out onto the street at this time? Maybe one of the memory ward inmates has escaped again. The figure is large and shambling, using a walker. They are also carrying something across the handles of the walker, but Bill can't see what it is until he is close enough for the street light to glint off gunmetal.

"Where in God's name have you been hiding a sawed-off shotgun?"

"Nobody rummages through an old man's underwear drawer."

Gilbert parks the walker and eases down next to him with a groan. He looks at Gil and waits. Gil faces forward, wheezing.

"I've always known there was another level to this that you were keeping me out of, based on the company you've been entertaining in the Game Room."

"Huh, didn't think anyone noticed," Bill replies.

"Obviously. Look, I'm no soldier, but us rural boys aren't strangers to guns or the occasional need to protect pride and property. When you've got two part-time deputies for an entire county, sometimes you have to look out for yourself."

Bill nods. "Alright, but I don't want to hear any bitching at breakfast. You've still got a chance to go back inside."

"This has got to be more interesting than checkers."

"Yes, and a lot more ..."

"Say, now, who is this a coming," Gil says softly, looking over Bill's shoulder and down the street.

Bill turns to look. A lone figure is strolling down the sidewalk, whistling. It is no one Bill recognizes. He stops and leans against the light pole, a genial expression on his face. He is wearing a T-shirt with a giant smiley face on it.

"Hello, gentleman. I am here with a message from the heads of the Covenant. Nice try. Impressively ambitious for a couple seniors, but you lose. Your friends are dead, your allies scattered, and the Covenant is secure."

The bottom falls out of Bill's stomach.

"Who is this joker?" demands Gil.

"I'm the head of Community and Social Services, the city department that manages this facility you live in, among other things."

Gil grunts. "You responsible for the food?"

"He's responsible for running a slaughterhouse," Bill replies. "He uses this place as a pipeline to provide," he pauses. The bureaucrat raises an eyebrow. "... provide subjects for illegal medical experiments. Ones they never come back from."

"He's the one, huh," Gil asks, voice flat.

The city official chuckles. "Close enough. Hopefully, my successor will be half as effective at running the system as I was. You see, I owe you thanks. When we got word of your daring plan, we moved the Mayor for his safety. He was on his way to my house when tragically a band of your assassins caught up to us and brutally murdered our dear leader."

The evil shit smirks.

"It's my duty to step up as Interim Mayor until the next election."

"You slimy son of a ..."

He raises a hand.

"Don't worry, it won't vex you for long. Oh, we're going to let you twist in the wind, see the fruits of your labor, attend your friends' funerals, and then one day soon it will be your turn to be ...," he smiles, "...medical subjects, knowing all the while how you failed and what really happens in this ..."

He never finishes, because Gilbert's shotgun barks and the dick wipe's head explodes.

"Jesus, that makes a mess," Gilbert whispers.

They both sit, stunned, then Gil shakes his head.

"Pretty sure I just made the world a better place." He reaches for the walker next to him and groans to his feet."

"Let's go see if there's any hot chocolate left in the kitchen."

23

BAD PENNY

They have all retreated into the dark, the Vampire Mayor waiting for news, the Secretary trying to glue her broken heart back together with the poison of revenge, and the Good Doctor scanning my blood to see if it is free of her toxin.

Death and I have been flirting for a long time, no, more like heavy petting. He's definitely had his hands under my clothes, whispering in my ear how sweet it is back at his place, how if I just give in, I'll finally be safe and at peace. Hunger makes the world go round, each, in our turn, devouring and being devoured, being the glutton and the feast. In some of us, the hunger is transmuted into the Need to be the meal. Let others try again and again to fill the void inside, let me be the satisfaction. I've worked to have that over and over again, to put off the final climax and following darkness. Preacher helped, as best he could. Having the Irregulars to come back to helped. Even the Good Doctor, in her fucked up way, helped. If it's time, I must make it count. Somehow I must take the vampire with me.

It will have to be soon. I'm already getting weak. Chained to the ceiling, alternating between the burning pain of hanging by my shoulders and the cramping of my calves when standing on my toes, dehydrated, and tortured by the Need emanating from my First Bite, I don't know how long my conscious mind can hold out before its all delirium and sensation.

I hear cell phones ring in the cavernous warehouse, distant conversations, tense sounding voices. Footsteps echo, but I can't tell where they come from or which direction they are moving. Finally, I hear what sounds like a group approaching. I start to be able to make out fragments of conversation.

"... did this happen?"

"The ... team failed ... never ... chance ... talked..."

Coming closer, the coldly furious voice of the Vampire Mayor. "I can not believe we are in danger here."

"They drove a garbage truck through the side of the other warehouse, Mayor."

They enter my circle of light. Two vampires and a human, all in suits, flank the Vampire Mayor. The Secretary and the Good Doctor trail behind at a discreet distance. One of the Vampire's lieutenants holds up a phone for his master to see.

"Pictures of the main entrance, where the guards made a stand."

The Vampire Mayor stops and takes the phone, staring at it in what looks like disbelief.

"How is this possible?"

"I told you to leave Preacher alone," I gloat.

He scowls. "You can't know this is him."

I do my best to leer at him knowingly. He hands the phone back to the vampire lieutenant.

"Just because they knew about that warehouse, doesn't mean they know about this one."

"I strongly suggest we relocate, Sir. Most of our men were concentrated at that location," the human servant speaks up. There's definitely fear in his voice.

"Yes, because that location was known, and therefore a more likely target. We knew an attack there was a possibility."

"Yes, Sir, but we never thought we would lose."

The Good Doctor speaks. "I'm not a soldier. I will not wait and see if we are attacked."

"You will do as I tell you, cattle."

"Very valuable cattle you do not want to waste," she replies, still ice. She returns his stare for an impressive couple seconds, before finally looking down at her shoes.

The Vampire Mayor growls in frustration. "Very well. We will retreat to the bunker for tonight and tomorrow." He nods at me. "Pack her up."

"There isn't time, Sir," the human flunky objects. I don't even see a blur of motion as the vampire breaks his neck.

"I will not be denied my prize," he roars.

"He was right," the Secretary says flatly. "Leave her. You can have fun hunting her down later with her precious preacher."

"She's too dangerous," the Good Doctor says. "We should kill her now."

No, it can't go this way. This is my only chance to make my death count. I bite down as hard as I can on the right side of my mouth. My new false tooth, paid for by the Vampire Mayor's administration, cracks into several pieces, which I swallow, along with the second dose of vampire poison I got from the Good Doctor. I can only hope that the amount the dentist could fit in the implant was enough. It's now or never, I must get him to bite me.

"How am I dangerous without your poison inside me, Doc?"

"Did you do the test? Was her blood clean?"

"Yes, it was free of the toxin, but ..."

Her voice, and all the rest, become a background buzzing. There is only him and me, the hunger and the need to be consumed. I have to be irresistible to him. With a rush of relief, I stop trying to ignore the burning, itching worms of fire crawling through my veins. I focus on their source, making the First Bite the center of my being. My body stretches taught in my chains, and I moan loudly. I can feel him responding, every predator's instinct reacting to my invitation. I let go of any control, of any sense of self beyond the Need, the need to be consumed, the need for it all to end. I beg with my whole body, with my whole being, for the ecstasy of annihilation. Then he is there, plunging his fangs into my neck. My body goes rigid, straining against chains, straining against gravity. I feel his desire to destroy, to consume, twin to my need to be consumed. Every nerve in my body screams with equal parts pleasure and pain. Our hearts beat in unison, pounding in time together, then finally beginning to slow. The ecstasy begins to shade into despair that the climax is over, that it can never be sustained. I feel him try to pull away, but I will not let him go. He struggles, screaming silently, but I wrap my soul around his, embracing the end, the final destruction, and we plunge together into nothingness.

***

There is an afterlife. After the darkness, comes gauzy, filtered light and distant voices. The faint voices, sometimes masculine, sometimes feminine, come and go. Occasionally there is a vague pressure, as if something is squeezing a phantom limb. When someone lifts my head and holds a glass of water to my mouth, which I am suddenly aware is very dry, a thought begins to swim through the murky depths of my mind.

"Am I alive?"

I'm not sure if I thought it or said it, so I repeat myself, trying to feel my mouth move.

"Am I alive?"

This time I hear the words in a croaking voice. The bed shifts as if someone moved, but it was not me. Oh, I am lying in bed. I can feel the weight of a blanket, and the mattress under me. Hard fingers brush hair away from my forehead, followed by a gentle kiss there.

"Yes, you are alive."

Forcing crusted eyelids open, I am met with the vision of two pieces of burning sea, framed by dark wings, hovering over me. I try to talk again but start coughing. Coughing hurts.

"Easy," Preacher says. He gently lifts my head and raises the glass of water to my lips.

"Sips at first, Penny. Your throat is learning how to work again."

I carefully swallow a few sips. He is still holding my head up and I look into his eyes.

"You always were good at training my throat."

He gets the slightly pained look he gets when I make an inappropriate joke during a serious moment. Like always, it is followed by a faint smile. He carefully lowers my head down onto my pillow. It is my pillow, my bed, my apartment.

"Apparently death and resurrection are not sufficient to make you less juvenile."

"Nope."

I am becoming aware of a dull ache from the left side of my neck that throbs with my pulse. Trying to raise an arm to feel it, Preacher stops me.

"All you will find is a large bandage. Best to leave it alone."

I feel it then, a ghost sensation of the Vampire Mayor savagely driving his fangs into me. The First Bite on my thigh tingles in sympathy.

"He really gnawed on me, huh?"

Preacher's face hardens into something very, very scary.

"We had to break his jaw with pliers to get his fangs out of you."

The hand still under my head trembles, and I can see the suffering underneath his anger.

"I'm sorry," I whisper.

"I will never forgive you."

"I know."

He kisses me as gently as a mother kisses her child. I manage to lift an arm and pull his head towards me until his mouth is mashing my lips against my teeth. I thrust my tongue into his wet, eager mouth, and then release him with a sigh, and settle back into the mattress. He stands up.

"You should rest."

Not until you tell me about the others."

I hold him there with my eyes, serious now. He sits back down on the chair that he has apparently been sitting in while watching over me.

"Your plan was betrayed, as you know. It's not known when the Secretary became a double agent, but she had apparently told the Vampire Mayor everything about the conspirators and the plan."

The hint of frustration in his voice, and the anger in his eyes, tells me she got away. I think I'm glad.

"Each of your planned attacks was therefore an ambush."

"You keep saying it like it was my plan. I just got roped into it at the last hour by those troublemakers."

"Do you want to hear what happened, or not?"

I nod, that small movement setting off little explosions of pain throughout my poor, abused body.

"The mafia woman who was to kill the human Mayor was gunned down by the remaining police loyal to him. Both she and her son died."

"The Wall is dead?"

"I understand he died well, trying to save his companions." The only time Preacher has ever spoken of him without derision.

"Was anyone else with them?"

"The other secretary, the one who is a Penny's Irregular. Both secretaries and Irregulars play an oddly large part in this plot."

"Is she OK?"

"Yes. She took a bullet to the shoulder, but managed to drive to safety with the mafia woman in the car, although it was too late for her."

"So that rat bastard is still Mayor."

"No."

"Huh?"

"What happened to him is a bit of a mystery. He disappeared on the way to a safe house. Most likely he was done away with by the underlings who were escorting him, one of which ended up with his head blown off outside a certain old folks home."

My still fuzzy brain was spinning. "Wait, so the Mayor escaped the hit, but was killed by his own people, some of whom ended up dead outside the Perfidus headquarters?"

"It was probably a coup. The escort who likely killed the Mayor and then lost his head, was the second in command, the head of Community Services."

He paused until I caught up.

"Oh, Jesus." Despite being an evil bastard, I'd kind of liked the Pretender.

"So who is running the city now?"

He chuckles, and I raise my eyebrows at him.

"Going to let me in on the joke?"

"Your Irregular, the former secretary, is Interim Mayor. There was complete panic at City Hall, and she stepped in and filled the void. Very level headed woman."

There is approval in his voice. It stings a little.

"That was the only part of the plan that completely succeeded. The human government is now firmly in the hands of the loyalists, as I am calling them. The vampire and police attempt to assassinate the Mafia Don was a failure. There were only a handful of vampires, and I suspect the gangsters have been developing countermeasures, despite being allied with them. They and their police allies were slaughtered."

He pauses to let me digest again.

"That leaves the Vampire Mayor," I almost whisper.

"He is quite dead," Preacher says, flatly. "Permanently, this time." The rage is creeping back in. "The vampires are in disarray, much like City Hall was, but they have not yet had a strong leader step in. Vampires are undisciplined by nature."

"Is that good or bad?"

He shrugs. "They return to their former, less subtle ways. They do more random damage, but perhaps less overall."

"And they are easier to hunt."

That calls a gleam into his eye.

"I have not yet had the opportunity."

For the first time, I feel a wave of guilt.

"Thank you for taking care of me. Again." I reach out and put a hand on his knee. He stares at my face, and I feel myself falling into those eyes.

"I have not been the only one. Sergio has also been your nursemaid, and sometimes Paul, a dishwasher from the Night Fowl. He brought his daughter, once. She is quite the little nurse."

"Sergio?" I remember something. "I heard something about a garbage truck?"

That gets another rare smile.

"Yes. You remember his job for the city. He was fearless when he drove that truck through the wall of the Vampire Mayor's warehouse."

"How many did you kill?"

"Less than I wanted to." That mask of rage again. "Which brings us to your other caretaker, the Good Doctor, you call her. She has been instrumental in keeping you alive."

"Really? Why did she help? I didn't think she was capable of remorse."

"She is not, but she does want to live."

"Ah."

"We have had some very instructive conversations. I have learned why she insisted on live subjects, despite the obvious danger. It seems that the results of studying the samples you brought her were confusing. It did not show that her poisons were effective, yet the vampires were dead."

"I don't understand. Of course, they were effective."

"The Good Doctor disagrees. She doesn't think her creations killed those vampires. She believes you did."

"That's ridiculous. How ..." My head is spinning. I remember the Vampire Mayor's heart beating in time with mine, slower and slower. I remember him trying to pull away, and wrapping my soul around his as we plunged into the abyss."

"I took them into the darkness with me."

"You returned. They did not."

"The pacemaker."

"Yes. For that, we still need the Doctor. You will require ongoing care. I have retained her services indefinitely."

He kisses me on the forehead and stands.

"Now you really do need to rest. I think you are strong enough for me to leave you on your own for just a little while. The Doctor will be here soon. She is very punctual."

He has his hand on the doorknob when I realize he has left someone out.

"What about Tommy? Was he a part of any of the attacks? Is he OK?"

He stops and looks back at me over his shoulder with a look I think is sympathy.

"Oh no."

"The car salesman is missing, despite a thorough search conducted by our new Mayor."

My stomach starts to ache, and I think I might cry.

"Bets have been placed on whether he is dead, or fled when the plan went awry. I have placed twenty dollars on flight. That one has the survival instincts of a rat."

***

God, I'm hungry. It's been two days since I regained consciousness and my appetite has gone from zero to a hundred and twenty. The Good Doctor has had me on a mostly liquid diet, but today I get a real breakfast. Sergio should be here with it any minute. When the knock comes, I'm so excited that I forget all security protocols and throw open the heavy door.

Her posture is just as perfect, and her head held just as high, but her clothes are dirty, her stockings torn, and her hair has escaped its tight bun. Her smell hits me just slightly later than the site of her. I start to slam the door but she takes a step forward and leans her shoulder against it.

"Penny, please. Give me one minute, then we will go if you want."

There is someone behind her in the hallway, someone I did not see until the Vampire Mayor's secretary moved. It is a young woman, a teenager by the looks of her. While the Secretary looks like someone recently cast into the street, this one has the exposed look of someone who has been there for a while. She's angry. It's telegraphed in every line of her body and swirls in her muddy brown eyes, Francis' eyes. I freeze, defensive instincts snuffed out.

"You recognize her. It is true, then."

"Francis must have shown me her picture a hundred times. But how ..."

"She says you're the reason. The reason the vampires came and killed my parents. Is it true?"

I can't look away from her face. Oh, Francis. I nod.

"Yes, it's true."

I think she is going to attack me. I can feel the coiled spring of violence in her, the girl who used to play the piano while her father listened from the other room. I make no move to defend myself, but the Secretary puts herself between us.

"You should let us in, don't you think?"

I meet her cool, triumphant gaze. I don't owe her anything, but I owe the girl everything. I step aside so they can come in. Today is a miracle.

Afterword

If you enjoyed the story, I would appreciate a short review on your preferred site. If you don't do reviews, tell a friend. It really does help. Thank you.

If you would like to hear more about Bad Penny, and keep up with my other work, you can subscribe to the newsletter at joshgentry.co m/newsletter.

ACKNOWLEDGEMENTS

I think your art is affected by everyone you've ever met. It used to be that when people asked a painter friend of mine how long it took her to paint a painting, she would answer with whatever age she was at the time. Well it took me 52 years to write this book, and I've met many people along the way. Some have had a bigger impact than others. My parents kicked it all off. They always supported me, from reading the naïve nature poems of a child to that time I got an English degree from the expensive school they were helping pay for. In those awkward high school years, making movies with friends and a camcorder showed me that having a creative outlet helped make it all bearable. You know who you are. I will never forget Ms. McDonald having us secretly read <u>Slaughterhouse-Five</u> in Advanced English, what a revelation. In college, one teacher had an outsized impact. After I had crashed and burned in my first poetry writing class, Beth Nugent gave me hope that I could maybe write a story, in her fiction class.

After college, I lost confidence and I stopped writing. As I found my way back to it many years later, there were some key figures. My siblings have always been great supporters. Jae gave me a rare blend of encouragement and brutal honesty that can't be overvalued. Suzy Mckee Charnas, a very fine author and person, took the time to read my work and treated it with respect.

Some people I haven't met but I feel like I have, also contributed to the existence of this book. I'm a devoted podcast listener, and I doubt that this book would exist without Mighty Mur Lafferty's, I Should Be Writing. On the publishing side of things, Joanna Penn's, The Creative Penn, has been invaluable.

All these people contributed to whatever is good in this book. Whatever is bad is all me.

About the Author

Josh Gentry lives in New Mexico and hopes the desert sun keeps the vampires away. Lamb is his favorite meat. He thinks, <u>The Vampire Tapestry</u>, is the most underrated vampire book. He has accepted that it is one space after periods, but will never accept zipper merging. The book trailer for Kiernan's, <u>The Drowning Girl</u>, is one of his favorite pieces of film. It only took him 52 years to write this book. Thank you for reading it.

www.joshgentry.com